MY LADY OF
THE CHIMNEY
CORNER

Alexander Irvine
MY LADY OF
THE CHIMNEY
CORNER

APPLETREE PRESS
BELFAST

First published in 1913 by Eveleigh Nash
This edition published in 1993 by
The Appletree Press Ltd
19-21 Alfred Street
Belfast BT2 8DL

Introduction copyright © Alistair J. Smyth, 1980
ISBN 0 86281 463 4 (de luxe)
ISBN 0 86281 464 2 (pbk)

Author's Note

This book is the torn manuscript of the most beautiful life I ever knew. I have merely pieced and patched it together, and have not even changed or disguised the names of the little group of neighbours who lived with us, at 'the bottom of the world'.

Contents

Introduction

In the face of brute poverty, semi-starvation and degradation, Anna Gilmore Irvine knew and understood and communicated the sustaining power of love. From her chimney corner she sent forth her light, a light which still burns, giving hope and courage to those who carry it. *My Lady of the Chimney Corner* is a tale of the faith, hope and charity that characterised a simple peasant woman's life. It is a story of pathos and rare spiritual beauty told simply and plainly; of the affection and reverence held by a son for his mother.

Alexander Fitzgerald Irvine lit a little candle from the light that shone from the chimney corner and carried it out. I retraced that pilgrimage in writing his biography—'Love is Enough'—What a life! What a strange circuitous pathway his was.

He was born near Pogue's Entry, Antrim, on 19th January, 1863. He was the ninth child of Anna and Jamie Irvine and the only one to be born in a caul: a thin, filmy veil covering the baby's head; a Celtic symbol of fortune.

As a boy he helped the fishermen on Lough Neagh, gathered scallops, willow sticks for thatching, ran errands, sold papers, played shinny, shot marbles, spun tops, went birdnesting and 'whistled from pillar to post with my hands in my pockets, with a tously head of red hair and scarcely enough clothing on me to dust a violin, a thing of shreds and patches, but dreaming—always dreaming'. Whèn a local landlord madé him a stable-boy, the introduction to respectability intensified the conflict between that dream of acquiring an education and his sense of duty:

Illiteracy was more than a handicap. It was a matter of shame. I had looked forward to being the support of my mother and father. That was one of my dreams; but spiritual quickening gave me discontent with ignorance. I felt that I must do something. To do it in Antrim seemed impossible. I must go away and shed my ignorance among strangers.

He turned his back on Antrim and made for Belfast. There he worked as a coachman and delivery boy but soon followed his brothers William, James and Dan to the coalmines of Scotland. He endured but loathed his work as a miner's mucker earning but a shilling a day. Ignorance and dirt seemed to be his lot in life. But in 1881 he joined the Royal Marine Corps that he might learn to read. The Mediterranean Fleet's flagship became his school. He learned quickly.

During this period he fell in love with and married an English girl, Ellen Mary Skeens. She bore him three sons: William Morris, Gordon Francis and Alexander Fitzgerald. After leaving the Marines, and spending a few months at Oxford University, he emigrated to the United States where he married his second wife. She bore him Robert Hazen, Maurice Harold, Jack Kingsley, and a daughter whom he christened Anna.

In 1888, Irvine began to 'plough fields for God' in the New York Bowery slums. His knowledge of men convinced him that men needed religion. Love of mankind was a fundamental thing in him. He was also convinced of his own need; but his growth was only to come through struggle; a progressive revelation of the Divine. From 1899 to 1903 he studied theology, taking his doctorate from the University of Yale, and afterwards carried his ministry from city slums to the pulpit of the grandly rich Church of the Ascension on New York's Fifth Avenue. Whereever he went, Dr Irvine never forgot his humble origin, and his affinity with the working classes developed in him the social reformer. His love for the ordinary working man carried him to the trenches of the First World War as a YMCA padre. He took there, to more than a million men, the philosophy Anna had given him:

I made men see through war to peace. I made of death a little thing and of life a great adventure. I kept my own body fit and efficient and when surfeited with slaughter of war and tired of soul I used it to keep my inner candle burning . . .

On the Somme during the war I used to look over toward Amiens every morning to see if the cathedral was still standing. One day I went over to the city. It was deserted, save for a few straggling citizens and some military policemen. Just beyond cavalry horses were clattering over the cobble stones as they passed on their way to the front. Emotions of awe, desolation, and reverence passed through my mind in quick succession. Incongruous world! sons of God, blowing each other to shreds. Two thousand years of teaching thrown to the winds, a denial of God and rejection of love.

I ensconced myself in a stall, closed my eyes, and comforted my soul in a daydream. 'After all,' I meditated, 'these heart-rending things are facts, but they are not realities. They are transitory. It is the unseen things that are real and eternal.' Then the 'fact' cathedral vanished in gray mist and a new cathedral took its place. Spectral figures of old friends of far away and long ago began to fill the stalls, the aisles and chapels. Saints stepped down from the pedestals and my spirit friends took their places. They had come from the ends of the earth, from gardens in the skies, from graves in Picardy, and from the palaces of the rich and the hovels of the poor. My new cathedral was a temple of friends.

I was awakened from my reverie by a gun barrage. A shell dropped on the west side and bespattered the walls and windows with splinters. The next might pierce the walls—how splendid, I thought, to go west from this bend in the road, on this leg of the journey! That night, in an uncomfortable dugout, wet and weary, I closed my eyes again and before me a second time passed my astral friends in a pageant of peace. Yes, this image-making faculty could be used anywhere and under all circumstances.

After his 'mind-sweeping' at the Front, Irvine was asked by Lloyd George to address the miners of Britain who had refused to return to work after the General Strike. The common man loved Irvine instinctively. Later, Irvine was elected to the National Executive of the American Socialist Party. But labour unions, and Irvine was an honorary member of six, were loathed by capitalists. The latter once had Irvine kidnapped and left for dead in the Californian desert. He survived, forgave, and loved his enemies.

He met and admired many great people, among them King George V and the Prince of Wales, Einstein, Madame Curie, General Gordon of Khartoum, William Butler Yeats, Mark Twain, 'O' Henry, Jack London, George Russell ('AE') and J.M. Barrie. But the greatest, and he never forgot it, was Anna.

What prompted him to write *My Lady of the Chimney Corner*, the tender and moving tribute to his mother?

I wanted to jot down some things in life that I was quite sure I believed. I passed in review the philosophical systems and sifted their meaning in the light of my experience. I recalled one after another of the many conceptions of God I had held. I scrutinised and analysed the political cures for our social evils.

Confronted with such a vast mass of conflicting opinions, what could the simple, unsophisticated soul do? Where would this dove of enquiry find rest for her feet? Where could the weary soul find peace?

To the sophisticated I am afraid my findings will seem childish, but they became to me a working formula. I knew it would have to be done over again, but there was an imperative demand for a philosophy of life at the time. What were the forces which dominated and motivated my life at the moment? They were personal, social, and spiritual. The love bond between my mother and myself, and mystical touch with Jesus, and the joy I experienced in helping men. Names, systems, theories, or creeds did not interest me. I wanted the facts. I wanted to be able to say, THIS I KNOW.

Sunk in direst poverty all her life, my mother in her chimney corner was a minister of light. Her sayings came to me with fresh meaning: 'There's only one kind of poverty, and that's to have no love in the heart'; 'God takes our hands and makes them His own to help folks'; 'A cup of sorrow is only half a cup when somebody shares it'. These and scores of other sayings had woven themselves into the texture of my being. When I was a barefooted boy selling newspapers on the streets of Antrim, I had an experience which gave me a thrill every time I thought of it. It was a cold night. My bare feet were bleeding. The cold wind penetrated my scant apparel. I looked up into the heavens and said, 'Jesus, if You will take my hand I shall not feel the cold'. Even as I sat there with a pencil in my hand I felt the thrill come back to me. That night I was warmed and illuminated. It was the nearest approach to the meaning of God that I ever had.

I determined to write a book on each of these sayings of my mother. In the face of poverty, when food was poor and scanty and our clothes in rags, my mother, in every respect but the material one, was a lady, and that is why I wrote her spiritual biography and called it, with a touch of irony, 'My Lady of the Chimney Corner'.

The old stone cabin down the cobbled Pogue's Entry just off Antrim's main street is preserved inviolate as a memorial to the Irvines, and next door is a little museum of Alexander's books and papers. The visitors' book there sports addresses from North America to South Australia. Dr Irvine returned there several times. About one of these visits, he recalled:

In the scenes of my childhood I seemed to be in another world. I was a stranger in the land of my birth. Everybody and everything seemed so small, so drab, so ancient. The door of our old stone cabin was like the gate of a public park—open to all comers. Folks of our neighbourhood walked in and out as people walk in and out of a department store. This was as I would have had it, up to a certain point. Then familiarity became something else. I wanted to be alone with my father and sister.

The chimney corner—my mother's place—was vacant. In all my life I have never felt an emptiness so keenly. She would have understood everything. My father and sister had not travelled far along the spiritual pathway of understanding. I went out to the potato field, to the spot from which the long pilgrimage started. I visited the stone pile where my childhood chum was breaking stones. He took the wire net from his eyes and looked at me. He expected me to look as I did when I left and talk in the old vernacular. He was disappointed in both. I was another person and he was the same. I expected some of the old fervour of companionship to return. There was no thrill, no common ground. A wide gulf separated us. It was of the mind.

I went to the churchyard and stood by the grave of the most saintly woman I have ever known—my mother. Everything I was and hoped to be I owed to her—to her love and faith. Perhaps she heard me as I said this at her grave.

Dr Irvine's final years were spent in a comfortable little bungalow in Mission Canyon at the back of the old Santa Barbara Mission, California. He enjoyed giving his attention to the beautiful garden and books he had acquired. At nearby Dean School he was the psychologist and dean of the chapel. Then, on 15th March 1941, he died. Five years later, his ashes were brought back to Pogue's Entry and laid to rest beside Anna and Jamie in the little graveyard of Antrim Parish Church.

Anna and Jamie, faced with the grave prejudices which curse Ulster to this day, found that love is enough; their son sends the maxim to us, his readers. When we come, one by one, to the twilight of life, may each of us feel able to say, as he did, 'I have done my bit, God, and here's your talent; I have multiplied it as best I could.'

Alastair J. Smyth,
Antrim.

Chapter 1

LOVE IS ENOUGH

'Anna's purty, an' she's good as well as purty, but th' beauty an' goodness that's hers is short lived, I'm thinkin',' said old Bridget McGrady to her neighbour Mrs Tierney, as Mrs Gilmore passed the door, leading her five-year-old girl, Anna, by the hand. The old women were sitting on the doorstep as the worshippers came down the lane from early mass on a summer morning.

'Thrue for you, Bridget, for th' do say that th' Virgin takes all sich childther before they're ten.'

'Musah, but Mrs Gilmore'll take on terrible,' continued Mrs Tierney, 'but th' will of God must be done.'

Anna was dressed in a dainty pink dress. A wide blue ribbon kept her wealth of jet black hair in order as it hung down her back, and the squeaking of her little shoes drew attention to the fact that they were new and in the fashion.

'It's a mortal pity she's a girl,' said Bridget, 'bekase she might hev been an althar boy before she goes.'

'Ay, but if she was a bhoy shure there's no tellin' what divilment she'd get into; so maybe it's just as well.'

The Gilmores lived on a small farm near Crumlin in County Antrim. They were not considered 'well-to-do', neither were they poor. They worked hard and by dint of economy managed to keep their children at school. Anna was a favourite child. Her quiet demeanour and gentle disposition drew to her many considerations denied the rest of the family. She was a favourite in the community. By the old women she was considered 'too good to live'; she took 'kindly' to the house of God. Her teacher said, 'Anna has a great head for learning.' This expression, oft repeated, gave the Gilmores an ambition to prepare Anna for teaching. Despite the schedule arranged for her, she was confirmed in the parish chapel at the age of ten. At fifteen she had exhausted the educational facilities of the community and set her heart on institutions of higher learning in the larger cities. While her parents were figuring that way the boys of the parish were figuring in a different direction. Before Anna was seventeen there was scarcely a boy living within miles who had not at one time or another lingered around the gate of the Gilmore garden. Mrs Gilmore watched Anna carefully. She warned her against the danger of an alliance with a boy of a lower station. The girl was devoted to the Church. She knew her *Book of Devotions* as few of the older people knew it, and before she was twelve she had read the *Lives of the Saints*. None of these things made her an ascetic. She could laugh heartily and had a keen sense of humour.

The old women revised their prophecies. They now spoke of her 'takin' th' veil'. Some said she would make 'a gey good schoolmisthress', for she was fond of children.

While waiting the completion of arrangements to continue her schooling, she helped her mother with the household work. She spent a good deal of her time, too, in helping the old and disabled of the village. She carried water to them from the village well and tidied up their cottages at least once a week.

The village well was the point of departure in many a romance. There the boys and girls met several times a day. Many a boy's first act of chivalry was to take the girl's place under the hoop that kept the cans apart and carry home the supply of water.

Half a century after the incident that played havoc with the dreams and visions of which she was the central figure, Anna said to me: 'I was fillin' my cans at th' well. He was standin' there lukin' at me.

' "Wud ye mind," says he, "if I helped ye?"

' "Deed no, not at all," says I.

'So he filled my cans an' then says he: "I would give you a nice wee cow if I cud carry thim home fur ye."

' "It's not home I'm goin'," says I, "but to an' oul' neighbour who can't carry it herself."

' "So much the better fur me," says he, an' off he walked between the cans.

'At Mary McKinstry's doore that afthernoon we stood till the shadows began t' fall.'

From the accounts rendered, old Mary did not lack for water-carriers for months after that. One evening Mary made tea for the water-carriers, and after tea she 'tossed th' cups' for them.

'Here's two roads, dear,' she said to Anna, 'an' wan day ye'll haave t' choose betwixt thim. On wan road there's love an' clane teeth (poverty), an' on t'other riches an' hell on earth.'

'What else do you see on the roads, Mary?' Anna asked.

'Plenty ov childther on th' road t' clane teeth, an' dogs an' cats on th' road t' good livin'.'

'What haave ye fur me, Mary?' Jamie Irvine,

Anna's friend, asked.

She took his cup, gave it a shake, looked wise, and said: 'Begorra, I see a big cup, me bhoy—it's a cup o' grief, I'm thinkin' it is.'

'Oul' Mary was jist bletherin',' he said, as they walked down the road in the gloaming, hand in hand.

'A cup of sorrow isn't so bad, Jamie, when there's two to drink it,' Anna said.

He pressed her hand tighter, and replied: 'Ay, that's thrue, fur then it's only half a cup.'

Jamie was a shoemaker's apprentice. His parents were very poor. The struggle for existence left time for nothing else. As the children reached the age of eight or nine they entered the struggle. Jamie began when he was eight. He had never spent a day at school. His family considered him fortunate, however, that he could be an apprentice.

The cup that old Mary saw in the tea-leaves seemed something more than 'blether' when it was noised abroad that Anna and Jamie were to be married.

The Gilmores strenuously objected. They objected because they had another career mapped out for Anna. Jamie was illiterate too and she was well educated. He was a Protestant and she an ardent Catholic. Illiteracy was common enough, and might be overlooked, but a mixed marriage was unthinkable.

The Irvines, on the other hand, although very poor, could see nothing but disaster in marriage with a Catholic, even though she was as 'pure and beautiful as the Virgin'.

'It's a shame an' a scandal,' others said, 'that a young fella who can't read his own name shud marry sich a nice girl wi' sich larnin'.'

Jamie made some defence, but it wasn't convincing.

'Doesn't the Bible say maan an' wife are wan?' he asked Mrs Gilmore in discussing the question with her.

'Ay.'

'Well, when Anna an' me are wan won't she haave a thrade, an' won't I haave an education?'

'That's wan way ov lukin' at a vexed question, but you're th' only wan that luks at it that way!'

'There's two,' Anna said. 'That's how I see it.'

When Jamie became a journeyman shoemaker, the priest was asked to perform the marriage ceremony. He refused, and there was nothing left to do but get a man who would give love as big a place as religion, and they were married by the vicar of the parish church.

Not in the memory of man in that community had a wedding created so little interest in one way and so much in another. They were both 'turncoats', the people said, and they were shunned by both sides. So they drank their first big draught of the 'cup o' grief' on their wedding-day.

'Sufferin' will be yer portion in this world,' Anna's mother told her, 'an' in th' world t' come separation from yer maan.'

Anna kissed her mother and said: 'I've made my choice, mother, I've made it before God, and as for Jamie's welfare in the next world, I'm sure that love like his would turn either Limbo, Purgatory, or Hell into a very nice place to live in!'

A few days after the wedding the young couple went out to the four crossroads. Jamie stood his staff on end and said: 'Are ye ready, dear?'

'Ay, I'm ready, but don't tip it in the direction of your preference!'

He was inclined toward Dublin, she toward Belfast. They laughed. Jamie suddenly took his hand from the staff and it fell, neither toward Belfast nor Dublin, but toward the town of Antrim, and toward Antrim they set out on foot. It was a distance of less than ten miles, but it was the longest journey she ever took—and the shortest, for she had all the world beside her, and so had Jamie. It was in June, and they had all the time there was. There was no hurry. They were as carefree as children, and utilised their freedom in full. Between Killead and Antrim they came to Willie Withero's stone-pile. Willie was Antrim's most noted stone-breaker in those days. He was one of the town's news centres. At his stone-pile he got the news going and coming. He was a strange mixture of philosophy and cynicism. He had a rough exterior, and spoke in short, curt, snappish sentences, but behind it all he had a big heart full of kindly human feeling.

'Anthrim's a purty good place fur pigs an' sich to live in,' he told the travellers. 'Ye see, pigs is naither Fenians nor Orangemen. I get along purty well m'self bekase I sit on both sides ov th' fence at th' same time.'

'How do you do it, Misther Withero?' Anna asked demurely.

'Don't call me "Misther",' Willie said: 'only quality calls me "Misther", an' I don't like it—it doesn't fit an honest stone-breaker.'

The question was repeated, and he said: 'I wear a green ribbon on Pathrick's Day an' an orange cockade on th' Twelfth ov July, an' if th' ax m' why, I tell thim t' go t' h—l! That's Withero for ye, an' wan ov 'im is enough for Anthrim, that's why I niver married, an' that'll save ye the trouble ov axin' me whither I've got a wife or no!'

'What church d'ye attend, Willie?' Jamie asked.

'Church is it, ye're axin' about? Luk here, me bhoy, step over th' stile.' Willie led the way over into the field.

'Step over here, me girl.' Anna followed.

A few yards from the hedge there was an ant-hill.

'See thim ants?'

'Ay.'

'Now if Withero thought thim ants hated aych other like th' men ov Anthrim, d'ye know what I'd do?'

'What?'

'I'd pour a kittle ov boilin' wather on thim an' roast the hides off ivery mother's son ov thim. Ay, that's what I'd do, shure as gun's iron!'

'That would be a sure and speedy cure,' Anna said, smiling.

'What's this world but an ant-hill?' he asked. 'Jist a big ant-hill, an' we're ants begorra an' uncles, but instead ov workin' like these wee fellas do—help aych other an' shouldther aych other's burdens, an' build up th' town, an' forage fur fodder, begobs we cut aych other's throats over th' colour of ribbon, or th' kind ov a church we attind! Ugh, what balderdash!'

The stone-breaker dropped on his knees beside the ant-hill and eyed the manoeuvring of the ants.

'Luk here!' he said.

They looked in the direction of his pointed finger and observed an ant dragging a dead fly over the hill.

'Jist watch that wee fella!'

They watched. The ant had a big job, but it pulled and pushed the big awkward carcass over the side of the hill. A second ant came along, sized up the situation, and took a hand. 'Ha, ha!' he chortled, 'that's th' ticket, now kape yer eye on him!'

The ants dragged the fly over the top of the hill and stuffed it down a hole.

'Now,' said Withero, 'if a fella in Anthrim wanted a han' th' other fellah wud say: 'Where d'ye hing yer hat up on Sunday?' or some other sich fool question!'

'He wud that.'

'Now mind ye, I'm not huffed at th' churches, aither Orange or Green, or th' praychers aither— tho' 'pon m' sowl, ivery time I luk at wan o' thim I think ov God as a first-class journeyman tailor! But I get more good switherin' over an ant-hill than whin wan o' thim wee praychers thry t' make me feel as miserable as th' divil!'

'There's somethin' in that,' Jamie said.

'Ay, ye kin bate a pair ov oul' boots there is!'

'What will th' ants do wi' th' fly?' Jamie asked.

'Huh!' he grunted, with an air of authority, 'they'll haave rump steaks fur tay and fly broth fur breakvist th' morra!'

'Th' don't need praychers down there, do th', Willie?'

'Don't need thim up here!' he said. 'They're signboards t' point th' way that iverybody knows as well as th' nose on his face!'

'Good-bye,' Anna said, as they prepared to leave.

'Good-bye, an' God save ye both kindly,' were Willie's parting words. He adjusted the wire protectors to his eyes and the sojourners went on down the road.

They found a mossy bank and unpacked their dinner.

'Quare, isn't he?' Jamie said.

'He has more sense than any of our people.'

'That's no compliment t' Withero, Anna, but I was jist thinkin' about our case; we've got t' decide somethin', an' we might as well decide it here as aanywhere.'

'About religion, Jamie?'

'Aye.'

'I've decided.'

'When?'

'At the ant-hill.'

'Ye cudn't be Withero?'

'No, dear, Willie sees only half th' world. There's love in it, that's bigger than colour of ribbon or creed of church. We've proven that, Jamie, haven't we?'

'But what haave ye decided?'

'That love is bigger than religion. That two things are sure. One is love of God. He loves all His children and gets huffed at none. The other is that the love we have for each other is of the same warp and woof as His for us, and *love is enough,* Jamie.'

'Ay, love is shure enough, an' enough's as good as a faste, but what about childther if th' come, Anna?'

'We don't cross a stile till we come to it, do we?'

'That's right, that's right, acushla; now we're as rich as lords, aren't we, but I'm th' richest, amn't I? I've got you and you've only got me.'

'I've got book learning, but you've got love and a trade, what more do I want? You've got more love than any man that ever wooed a woman—so I'm richer, amn't I?'

'Oh, God,' Jamie said, 'but isn't this th' lovely world, eh, Anna?'

26

Within a mile of Antrim they saw a cottage perched on a high bluff by the road side. It was reached by stone steps. They climbed the steps to ask for a drink of water. They were kindly received. The owner was a follower of Wesley, and his conversation at the well was in sharp contrast to the philosophy at the stone-pile. The young journeyman and his wife were profoundly impressed with the place. The stone cottage was vine clad. There were beautiful trees and a garden. The June flowers were in bloom and a cow grazed in the pasture near by.

'Some day we'll haave a home like this,' Jamie said, as they descended the steps.

Anna named it 'The Mount of Temptation', for it was the nearest she had ever been to the sin of envy. A one-armed Crimean pensioner named Steele occupied it during my youth. It could be seen from Pogue's Entry, and Anna used to point it out and tell the story of that memorable journey. In days when clouds were heavy and low and the gaunt wolf stood at the door, she would say: 'Do you mind the journey to Antrim, Jamie?'

'Ay,' he would say, with a sigh, 'an' we've been in love ever since, haven't we, Anna?'

Chapter 2

THE WOLF AND THE CARPENTER

For a year after their arrival in Antrim they lived in the home of the master shoemaker for whom Jamie worked as a journeyman. It was a great hardship, for there was no privacy, and their daily walk and conversation, in front of strangers, was of the 'yea, yea' and 'nay, nay' order. In the summer-time they spent their Sundays on the banks of Lough Neagh, taking whatever food they needed and cooking it on the sand. They continued their courting in that way. They watched the waterfowl on the great wide marsh, they waded in the water and played as children played. In more serious moods she read to him Moore's poems and went over the later lessons of her school life. Even with but part of a day in each week together they were very happy. The world was full of sunshine for them then. There were no clouds, no regrets, no fears. It was a period—a brief period—that for the rest of their lives they looked back upon as a time when they really lived. I am not sure, but I am of the impression that the chief reason she could not be persuaded to visit the Lough in later life was because she wanted to remember it as she had seen it in that first year of their married life.

The first child was two years of age when the famine came—the famine that swept over Ireland like a plague, leaving in its wake over a million new-made graves. They had been in their own house for over a year. It was scantily furnished, but it was *home*. As the ravages of the famine spread, nearly every family in the town mourned the absence of some member. Men and women met on the street one day, were gone the next. Jamie put his bench to one side and sought work at anything he could get to do. Prices ran up beyond the possibilities of the poor. The potato crop only failed. The other crops were reaped and the proceeds sent to England as rent and interest, and the reapers having sent the last farthing, lay down with their wives and children and died. Of the million who died, four hundred thousand were able-bodied men. The wolf stood at every door. The carpenter alone was busy. Of course, it was the poor who died—the poor only. In her three years of married life Anna realised in a measure that the future held little change for her or her husband, but she saw a ray of hope for the boy in the cradle. When the foodless days came and the child was not getting food enough to survive, she gave vent to her feelings of despair. Jamie did not quite understand when she spoke of the death of hope.

'Spake what's in yer heart plainly, Anna!' he said plaintively.

'Jamie, we must not blame each other for anything, but we must face the fact—we live at the bottom of the world where every hope has a headstone—a headstone that only waits for the name.'

'Ay, dear, God help us, I know, I know what ye mane.'

'Above and beyond us,' she continued, 'there is a world of nice things—books, furniture, pictures—a world where people and things can be kept clean, but it's a world we could never reach. But I had hope—'

She buried her face in her hands and was silent.

'Ay ay, acushla, I know yer hope's in the boy, but don't give up. We'll fight it out together if th' worst comes to th' worst. The boy'll live, shure he will!'

He could not bear the agony on her face. It distracted him. He went out and sought solitude on a pile of stones at the back of the house. There was no solitude there, nor could he have remained long if there had been. He returned, and drawing a stool up close beside her, he sat down and put an arm tenderly over her shoulder.

'Cheer up, wee girl,' he said, 'our ship's comin' in soon.'

'If we can only save him!' she said, pointing to the cradle.

'Well, we won't cry over spilt milk, dear—not at laste until it's spilt.'

'Ah,' she exclaimed, 'I had such hopes for him!'

'Ay, so haave I, but thin again I've thought t' myself, suppose th' wee fella did get t' be kind-a quality like, wudn't he be ashamed ov me an' you maybe, an' shure an ingrate that's somethin' is worse than nothin'!'

'A child born in pure love couldn't be an ingrate, Jamie; that isn't possible, dear.'

'Ah, who knows what a chile will be, Anna?'

The child awoke and began to cry. It was a cry for food. There was nothing in the house; there had been nothing all that day. They looked at each other. Jamie turned away his face. He arose and left the house. He went aimlessly down the street, wondering where he should try for something to eat for the child. There were several old friends whom he supposed were in the same predicament, but to whom he had not appealed. It was getting to be an old story. A score of as good children as his had been buried. Everybody was polite, full of sympathy, but the child was losing his vitality, so was the mother. Something desperate must be done, and done at once. For the third time he importuned a grocer at whose shop he had spent much money. The grocer was just putting up the window shutters for the night.

'If ye cud jist spare us a ha'p'orth ov milk to keep th' life in th' chile fur th' night?' he pleaded.

'It wouldn't be a thimbleful if I had it, Jamie, but I haven't—we haave childther ov our own, ye know, an' life is life!'

'Ay ay,' he said, 'I know, I know,' and shuffled out again. Back to the house he went. He lifted the latch gently and tip-toed in. Anna was rocking the child to sleep. He went softly to the table and took up a tin can and turned again toward the door.

Anna divined his stealthy movement. She was beside him in an instant.

'Where are you going, Jamie?'

He hesitated. She forced an answer.

'Jamie,' she said in a tone new to her, 'there's been nothing but truth and love between us; I must know.'

'I'm goin' out wi' that can to get somethin' fur the chile, Anna, if I haave t' swing fur it. That's what's in my mind, an' God help me!'

'God helped us both,' she said.

He moved toward the street. She planted herself between him and the door.

'No, we must stand together. They'll put you in jail, and then the child and I will die anyway. Let's wait another day!'

They sat down together in the corner. It was dark now, and they had no candle. The last handful of

31

turf was on the fire. They watched the sparks play and the fitful spurts of flame light up for an instant at a time the darkened home. It was a picture of despair—the first of a long series that ran down the years with them. They sat in silence for a long time. Then they whispered to each other with many a break the words they had spoken in what now seemed to them the long ago. The fire died out. They retired, but not to sleep. They were too hungry. There was an insatiable gnawing at their vitals that made sleep impossible. It was like a cancer with excruciating pain added. Sheer exhaustion only stilled the cries of the starving child. There were no more tears in their eyes, but anguish has by-valves more keen, poignant, and subtle.

In agony they lay in silence and counted time by the repercussion of pain until the welcome dawn came with its new supply of hope. The scream of a frenzied mother who had lost a child in the night was a prelude to a tragic day. Anna dressed quickly and in a few minutes stood by the side of the woman. There was nothing to say. Nothing to do. It was her turn. It would be Anna's next. All over the town the spectre hovered. Every day the reaper garnered a new harvest of human sheaves. Every day the wolf barked. Every day the carpenter came.

When Anna returned Jamie had gone. She took her station by the child. Jamie took the tin can and went out along the Graystone Road for about a mile, and entered a pasture where three cows were grazing. He was weak and nervous. His eyes were bloodshot and his hands trembled. He had never milked a cow. He had no idea of the difficulty involved in catching a cow and milking her in a pasture. There was the milk and yonder his child, who, without it, would not survive the day. Desperation dominated and directed every movement.

The cows walked away as he approached. He followed. He drove them into a corner of the field and managed to get his hand on one. He tried to pet her, but the jingling of the can frightened her and off they went—all of them—on a fast trot along the side of the field. He became cautious as he cornered them a second time. This time he succeeded in reaching an udder. He got a tit in his hand. He lowered himself to his haunches and proceeded to tug vigorously. His hand was waxy and stuck as if glued to the flesh. Before there was any sign of milk the cow gave him a swift kick that sent him flat on his back. By the time he pulled himself together again the cows were galloping to the other end of the pasture.

'God!' he muttered, as he mopped the sweat from his face with his sleeve, 'if ye've got aany pity or kindly feelin' giv' me a sup ov that milk for m' chile! Come on!'

His legs trembled so that he could scarcely stand. Again he approached. The cows eyed him with sullen concern. They were thoroughly scared now, and he couldn't get near enough to lay a hand on any of them. He stood in despair, trembling from head to foot. He realised that what he would do he must do quickly.

The morning had swift wings—it was flying away. Some one would be out for the cows ere long, and his last chance would be gone. He dropped the can and ran to the farm-house. There was a stack-yard in the rear. He entered and took a rope from a stack. It was a long rope—too long for his use, but he did not want to destroy its usefulness. He dragged it through the hedge after him. This time with care and caution he got near enough to throw the rope over the horns of a cow. Leading her to a fence, he tied her to it and began again. It came slowly. His strength was almost gone. He went from one side to the other—now at one tit, now at another. From his haunches he went to his knees, and from that position he stretched out his legs and sat flat on the grass. He no sooner had a good position than the cow would change hers. She trampled on his legs and swerved from side to side, but he held on. It was a life and death struggle. The little milk at the bottom of the can gave him strength and courage. As he literally pulled it out of her, his strength increased. When the can was half full he turned the cow loose and made for the gap in the hedge. Within a yard of it he heard a loud report of a gun, and the can dropped to the ground. The ball had ploughed through both lugs of the can, disconnecting the wire handle. Not much of the milk was lost. He picked up the can and started down the road as fast as his legs could take him. He had only gone a hundred yards when a man stepped out into the road and levelled a gun at him.

'Another yard an' I'll blow your brains out!' the man said.

'Is this yer milk?' Jamie asked.

'Ay, an' well ye know it's m' milk!'

Jamie put the can down on the road and stood silent. The farmer delivered himself of a volume of profane abuse. Jamie did not reply. He stood with his head bowed and to all appearances in a mood of penitence.

When the man finished his threats and abuse he stooped to pick up the can. Before his hand touched it Jamie sprang at him with the ferocity of a panther.

34

There was a life and death tussle for a few seconds, and both men went down on the road—Jamie on top. Sitting on the man's chest he took a wrist in each hand and pinned him to the ground.

'Ye think I'm a thief,' he said to the man, as he looked at him with eyes that burned like live coals. 'I'm not, I'm an honest man, but I haave a chile dying wi' hunger—now it's your life or his, by —— an' ye'll decide!'

'I think yer a liar as well as a thief,' the man said, 'but if ye can prove what ye say, I'm yer friend.'

'Will ye go with me?'

'Ay.'

'D'ye mane it?'

'Ay, I do!'

'I'll carry th' gun.'

'Ye may, there's nothin' in it.'

'There's enough in th' butt t' batther a maan's brains out.'

Jamie seized the gun and the can and the man got up.

They walked down the road in silence, each watching the other out of the corners of his eyes.

'D'ye believe in God?' Jamie asked abruptly. The farmer hesitated before answering.

'Why d'ye ask?'

'I'd like t' see a maan in these times that believed wi' his heart insted ov his mouth.'

'Wud he let other people milk his cows?' asked the man sneeringly.

'He mightn't haave cows t' milk,' Jamie said. 'But he'd be kind and not a glutton!'

They arrived at the house. The man went in first. He stopped near the door, and Jamie instinctively and in fear shot past him. What he saw dazed him.

'Ah, God!' he exclaimed. 'She's dead!'

Anna lay on her back on the floor and the boy was asleep by the hearth with his head in the ashes. The neighbours were alarmed, and came to assist. The farmer felt Anna's pulse. It was feebly fluttering.

'She's not dead,' he said. 'Get some cold wather quickly!'

They dashed the water in her face and brought her back to consciousness. When she looked around, she said: 'Who's this kind man come in to help, Jamie?'

'He's a farmer,' Jamie said, 'an' he's brot ye a pint ov nice fresh milk!' The man had filled a cup with milk and put it to Anna's lips.

She refused. 'He's dying,' she said, pointing to the boy, who lay limp on the lap of a neighbour.

The child was drowsy and listless. They gave him the cup of milk; he had scarcely enough strength to drink. Anna drank what was left, which was very little.

'God bless you!' Anna said, as she held out her hand to the farmer.

'God save you kindly,' he answered, as he took her hand and bowed his head. 'I've a wife an' wains myself,' he continued, 'but we're not s' bad off on a farm.' Turning to Jamie he said: 'Yer a Protestant!'

'Ay.'

'An' I'm a Fenian, but we're in th' face ov bigger things!'

He extended his hand. Jamie clasped it, the men looked into each other's faces and understood.

That night in the dusk, the Fenian farmer brought a sack of potatoes and a quart of fresh milk, and the spark of life was prolonged.

Chapter 3

REHEARSING FOR THE SHOW

Famine not only carried off a million of the living, but it claimed also the unborn. Anna's second child was born a few months after the siege was broken, but the child had been starved in its mother's womb, and lived only three months. There was no wake. Wakes are for older people. There were no candles to burn, no extra sheet to put over the old dresser, and no clock to stop at the moment of death.

The little wasted thing lay in its undressed pine coffin on the table, and the neighbours came in and had a look. Custom said it should be kept the allotted time, and the tyrant was obeyed. A dozen of those to whom a wake was a means of change and recreation, came late and planted themselves for the night.

'Ye didn't haave a hard time wi' th' second, did ye, Anna?' asked Mrs Mulholland.

'No,' Anna said quietly.

'The hard times play'd th' divil wi' it before it was born, I'll be bound,' said a second.

A third averred that the child was 'the very spit of its father's mouth.' Ghost stories, stories of the famine, of hard luck, of hunger, of pain, and the thousand and one aspects of social and personal sorrow had the changes rung on them.

Anna sat in the corner. She had to listen, she had to answer when directly addressed, and the prevailing idea of politeness made her the centre of every story and the object of every moral.

The refreshments were all distributed and diplomatically the mourners were informed that there was nothing more; nevertheless they stayed on and on. Nerve-racked and unstrung, Anna staggered to her feet and took Jamie to the door.

'I'll go mad, dear, if I have to stand it all night!'

They dared not be discourteous. A reputation for heartlessness would have followed Anna to the grave if she had gone to bed while the dead child lay there.

Withero had been at old William Farren's wake, and was going home when he saw Anna and Jamie at the door. They explained the situation.

'Take a dandther down toward th' church,' he said 'an' then come back.'

Willie entered the house in an apparently breathless condition.

'Yer takin' it purty aisy here,' he said, 'whin' 'Jowler' Hainey's killin' his wife an' wreckin' th' house!'

In about two minutes he was alone. He put a coal in his pipe and smoked for a minute. Then he went over to the little coffin. He took the pipe out of his mouth, laid it on the mantel-shelf, and returned. The little hands were folded. He unclasped them, took one of them in his rough, calloused palm.

'Poore wee thing,' he said in an undertone, 'poore wee thing.' He put his hands as he found them. Still looking at the little baby face, he added: 'Heigho, heigho, it's bad, purty bad, but it's worse where there isn't even a dead wan!'

When Anna returned she lay down on her bed, dressed as she was, and Jamie and Withero kept the vigil—with the door barred. Next morning at the earliest respectable hour, Withero carried the little coffin under his arm, and Jamie walked beside him to the graveyard.

During the fifteen years that followed the burial of 'the famine child' they buried three others and saved three—four living and four dead.

I was the ninth child. Anna gave me a Greek name, which means 'Helper of men'. Shortly after my arrival in Scott's Entry, they moved to Pogue's Entry. The stone cabin was thatch-covered, and measured about twelve by sixteen feet. The space comprised three compartments. One, a bedroom; over the bedroom and beneath the thatch a little loft that served as a bedroom to those of climbing age. The rest of it was workshop, dining-room, sitting-room, parlour, and general community news centre. The old folks slept in a bed, the rest of us slept on the floor and beneath the thatch. Between the bedroom door and the open fireplace was the chimney-corner. Near the door stood an old pine table and some dressers. They stood against the wall and were filled with crockery. We never owned a chair. There were several pine stools, a few creepies (small stools), and a long bench that ran along the bed-room wall, from the chimney-corner to the bedroom door. The mud floor never had the luxury of a covering, nor did a picture ever adorn the bare walls. When the floor needed patching, Jamie went to somebody's garden, brought a shovelful of earth, mixed it and filled the holes. The stools and creepies were scrubbed once a week, the table once a day. I could draw an outline of that old table now and accurately mark every dent and crack in it. I do not know where it came from, but each of us had a *hope* that one day we would possess a pig. We built around the hope a sty and placed it against the end of the cabin. The pig never turned up, but the hope lived there throughout a generation!

We owned a goat once. In three months it reduced the smooth kindly feeling in Pogue's Entry to the point of total eclipse. We sold it and spent a year in winning back old friends. We had a garden. It measured thirty-six by sixteen inches, and was just outside the front window. At one end was a small currant bush and in the rest of the space Anna grew an annual crop of nasturtiums.

Once we were prosperous. That was when two older brothers worked with my father at shoe-making. I remember them, on winter nights, sitting around the big candlestick—one of the three always singing folk-songs as he worked. As they worked near the window, Anna sat in her corner and by the light of a candle in her little sconce made waxed ends for the men. I browsed among the lasts, clipping, cutting, and scratching old leather parings and dreaming of the wonderful days beyond when I too could make a boot and sing 'Black-eyed Susan'.

Then the news came—news of a revolution.

'They're making boots by machinery now,' Anna said one day.

'It's dotin' ye are, Anna,' Jamie replied. She read the account.

'How cud a machine make a boot, Anna?' he asked in bewilderment.

'I don't know, dear.'

Barney McQuillan was the village authority on such things. When he told Jamie, he looked aghast, and said, 'How quare!'

The makers became menders—shoemakers became cobblers. There was something of magic and romance in the news that a machine could turn out as much work as twenty-five men, but when my brothers moved away to other parts of the world to find work, the romance was rubbed off.

'Maybe we can get a machine?' Jamie said.

'Ay, but shure ye'd have to get a factory to put it in!'

'Is that so?'

'Ay, an' we find it hard enough t' pay fur what we're in now!'

Barney McQuillan was the master shoemaker in our town who was best able to readjust himself to changed conditions. He became a master-cobbler and doled out what he took in to men like Jamie. He kept a dozen men at work, making a little off each, just as the owner of the machine did in the factory. In each case the need of skill vanished, and the power of capital advanced. Jamie dumbly took what was left—cobbling for Barney. To Anna the whole thing meant merely the death of a few more hopes. For over twenty years she had fought a good fight, a fight in which she played a losing part, though she was never wholly defeated.

Her first fight was against slang and slovenly speech. She started early in their married life to correct Jamie. He tried hard and often, but he found it difficult to speak one language to his wife and another to his customers. From the lips of Anna it sounded all right, but the same pronunciation by Jamie seemed affected, and his customers gaped at him.

Then she directed her efforts anew to the children. One after another she corrected their grammar and pronunciation, corrected them every day and every hour of the day that they were in her presence. Here again she was doomed to failure. The children lived on the street and spoke its language. It seemed a hopeless task. She never whined over it. She was too busy cleaning, cooking, sewing and at odd times helping Jamie, but night after night for nearly a generation she took stock of a life's effort and each milestone on the way spelt failure. She could see no light—not a glimmer. Not only had she failed to impress her language upon others, but she found herself gradually succumbing to her environment, and lapsing into vulgar forms herself. There was a larger and more vital conflict than the one she had lost. It was the fight against dirt. In such small quarters, with so many children and such activity in work, she fought against great odds. Bathing facilities were almost impossible: water had to be brought from the town well, except what fell on the roof, and that was saved for washing clothes. Whatever bathing there was, was done in the tub in which Jamie steeped his leather.

We children were suspicious that when Jamie bathed Anna had a hand in it. They had a joke between them that could only be explained on that basis. She called it 'grooming the elephant'.

'Jist wait, m' boy,' she would say in a spirit of kindly banter, 'till the elephant has to be groomed, and I'll bring ye down a peg or two.'

There was a difference of opinion among them as to the training of children.

'No chile iver thrived on saft words,' he said; 'a wet welt is betther.'

'Ay, yer wet welt stings th' flesh, Jamie, but it niver gets at a chile's mind.'

'Thrue for you, but who th' —— kin get at a chile's mind?'

42

One day I was chased into the house by a bigger boy. I had found a farthing. He said it was his. The money was handed over and the boy left with his tongue in his cheek. I was ordered to strip. When ready, he laid me across his knee and applied the 'wet welt'.

An hour later it was discovered that a week had elapsed between the losing and finding of the farthing. No sane person would believe that a farthing could lie for a whole week on the streets of Antrim.

'Well,' he said, 'ye need a warmin' like that ivery day, an' ye had nown yestherday, did ye?'

On another occasion I found a ball, one that had never been lost. A boy, hoping to get me in front of my father, claimed the ball. My mother on this occasion sat in judgment.

'Where did *you* get the ball?' she asked the boy. He couldn't remember. She probed for the truth, but neither of us would give in. When all efforts failed she cut the ball in half and gave each a piece!

'Nixt time I'll tell yer Dah,' the boy said, when he got outside, 'he makes you squeal like a pig.'

When times were good—when work and wages got a little ahead of hunger, which was seldom, Anna baked her own bread. Three kinds of bread she baked. 'Soda'—common flour bread, never in the shape of a loaf, but bread that lay flat on the girdle; 'pirta oaten'—made of flour and oatmeal; and 'fadge'—potato bread. She always sung while baking, and she sang the most melancholy and plaintive airs. As she baked and sang, I stood beside her on a creepie, watching the process and awaiting the end, for at the close of each batch of bread I always had my 'duragh'—an extra piece.

When hunger got ahead of wages, the family

bread was bought at Sam Johnston's bakery. The journey to Sam's was full of temptation to me. Hungry and with a vested interest in the loaf on my arm I was not over punctilious in details of the moral law. Anna pointed out the opportunities of such a journey. It was a chance to try my mettle with the arch temper. It was a mental gymnasium in which moral muscle got strength. There wasn't in all Ireland a mile of highway so well paved with good intentions. I used to start out, well keyed up morally and humming over and over the order of the day. When, on the home stretch, I had made a dent in Sam's architecture, I would lay the loaf down on the table, good side toward my mother. While I was doing that she had read the story of the fall on my face. I could feel her penetrating gaze.

'So he got ye, did he?'

'Ay,' I would say in a voice too low to be heard by my father.

The order at Sam's was usually a sixpenny loaf, three ha'pence worth of tea and sugar, and half an ounce of tobacco.

There were times when Barney had no work for my father, and on such occasions I came home empty-handed. Then Jamie would go out to find work as a day-labourer. Periods like these were glossed over by Anna's humour and wit. As they sat around the table, eating 'stir-about' without milk, or bread without tea, Jamie would grunt and complain.

'Ay, faith,' Anna would say, 'it's purty bad, but it's worse where there's none at all.'

When the wolf lingered long at the door I went foraging—foraging as forages a hungry dog and in the same places. Around the hovels of the poor, where dogs have clean teeth a boy has little chance.

One day, having exhausted the ordinary channels of relief without success, I betook myself to the old swimming-hole on the mill race.The boys had a custom of taking a 'shiverin' bite' when they went bathing. It was on a Sunday afternoon in July, and quite a crowd sat around the hole. I neither needed nor wanted a bath—I wanted a bite. No one offered a share of his crust. A big boy named Healy was telling of his prowess as a fighter.

'I'll fight ye fur a penny!' said I.

'Where's yer penny?' said Healy.

'I'll get it th' morra.'

A man, seeing the difficulty and willing to invest in a scrap, advanced the wager. I was utterly outclassed and beaten. Peeling my clothes off I went into the race for a swim and to wash the blood off. When I came out Healy had hidden my trousers. I searched for hours in vain. The man who paid the wager gave me an extra penny and I went home, holding my jacket in front of my legs. The penny saved me from a 'warming', but Anna, feeling that some extra discipline was necessary, made me a pair of trousers out of an old potato-sack.

'That's sackcloth, dear,' she said, 'an' ye can aither sit in th' ashes in them or wear them in earning another pair! Hold fast t' yer penny!'

In this penitential outfit I had to sell my papers. Every fibre of my being tingled with shame and humiliation. I didn't complain of the penance, but I swore vengeance on Healy. She worked the desire for vengeance out of my system in her chimney-corner by reading to me often enough, so that I memorised the fifty-third chapter of Isaiah. Miss McGee, the postmistress, gave me sixpence for the accomplishment, and that went toward a new pair of trousers. Concerning Healy, Anna said: 'Bate 'im with a betther brain, dear!'

Despite my fistic encounters, my dents in the family loaves, my shinny, my marbles, and the various signs of total, or at least partial, depravity, Anna clung to the hope that out of this thing might finally come what she was looking, praying, and hoping for.

An item on the credit side of my ledger was that I was born in a caul—a thin, filmy veil that covered me at birth. Of her twelve I was the only one born in 'luck'. In a little purse she kept the caul, and on special occasions she would exhibit it and enumerate the benefits and privileges that went with it. Persons born in a caul were immune from being hung, drawn, and quartered, burned to death, or lost at sea.

It was on the basis of the caul I was rented to old Mary McDonagh. My duty was to meet her every Monday morning. The meeting insured her luck for the week. Mary was a huckster. She carried her shop on her arm—a wicker basket in which she had thread, needles, ribbons, and other things, which she sold to the farmers and folks away from the shopping centre. No one is lucky while bare-footed. Having no shoes, I clattered down Sandy Somerville's entry to my father's. At the first clatter, she came out, basket on arm, and said: 'Morra, bhoy, God's blessin' on ye!'

'Morra, Mary, an' good luck t' ye,' was my answer.

I used to express my wonder that I couldn't turn this luck of a dead-sure variety into a pair of shoes for myself.

Anna said: 'Yer luck, dear, isn't in what ye can get,

but in what ye can give!'

When Antrim opened its first flower show, I was a boy of all work at old Mrs Chaine's. The gardener was pleased with my work and gave me a hothouse plant to put in competition. I carried it home proudly and laid it down beside her in the chimney-corner.

'The gerd'ner says it'll bate th' brains out on aany geranium in the show!' I said.

'Throth it will that, dear,' she said, 'but sure ye couldn't take a prize fur it!'

'Why?' I growled.

'Ah, honey, shure everybody would know that ye didn't grow it—forby they know that th' smoke in here would kill it in a few days.'

I sulked and protested.

'That's a nice way t' throw cowld wather on th' chile,' Jamie said.'Why don't ye let 'im go on an' take his chances at the show?'

A pained look overspread her features. It was as if he had struck her with his fist. Her eyes filled with tears, and she said huskily: 'The whole world's a show, Jamie, an' this is the only place the wee fella has to rehearse in.'

I sat down beside her and laid my head in her lap. She stroked it in silence for a minute or two. I couldn't quite see, however, how I could miss that show! She saw that after all I was determined to enter the lists. She offered to put a card on it for me, so that they would know the name of the owner. This is what she wrote on the card: 'This plant is lent for decorative purposes.'

That night there was an unusual atmosphere in her corner. She had a newly-tallied cap on her head and her little Sunday shawl over her shoulders. Her candle was burning and the hearthstones had an extra coat of whitewash. She drew me up close beside her and told me a story.

'Once, a long, long time ago, God, feelin' tired, went to sleep, an' had a nice wee nap on His throne. His head was in His han's, an' a wee white cloud came down an' covered Him up. Purty soon He wakes up, and says He: 'Where's Michael?'

' "Here I am, Father!"

' "Michael, me boy," says God, "I want a chariot and a charioteer!"

' "Right ye are!" says he. Up comes the purtiest chariot in the City of Heaven an' finest charioteer.

' "Me boy,' says God, 'take a million tons ov th' choicest seeds of th' flowers of Heaven an' take a trip around th' world wi' them. Scatther them," says He, "be th' roadsides an' th' wild places of th' earth where my poor live."

' "Ay," says the charioteer, "that's jist like ye, Father. It's th' purtiest job of m' afther-life, an' I'll do it finely."

' "It's jist come t' Me in a dream," says th' Father, "that th' rich have all the flowers down there and th' poor haave nown at all. If a million tons isn't enough take a billion tons!" '

At this point I got in some questions about God's language and the kind of flowers.

'Well, dear,' she said, 'He spakes Irish t' Irish people, and the charioteer was an Irishman.'

'Maybe it was a wuman!' I ventured.

'Ay, but there's no difference up there.'

'Th' flowers,' she said, 'were primroses, butthercups, an' daisies, an' th' flowers that be handy t' th' poor, an' from that day to this there's been flowers aplenty for all of us everywhere!

'Now you go to-morra an' gether a basketful, an' we'll fix them up in th' shape of th' Pyramid of Egypt, an' maybe we'll get a prize.'

I spent the whole of the following day, from dawn to dark, roaming over the wild places near Antrim gathering the flowers of the poor. My mother arranged them in a novel bouquet—a bouquet of wild flowers, the base of it yellow primroses, the apex of pink shepherd's sundials, and between the base and the apex one of the greatest variety of wild flowers ever gotten together in that part of the world.

It created a sensation and took first prize. At the close of the exhibition Mrs James Chaine distributed the prizes. When my name was called I went forward slowly, blushing in my rags, and received a twenty-four piece set of china! It gave me a fit! I took it home, put it in her lap, and danced. We held open house for a week, so that every man, woman, and child in the community could come in and 'handle' it.

Withero said we ought to save up and build a house to keep it in!

She thought that a propitious time to explain the inscription she put on the card.

'Ah, thin,' I said, 'shure it's thrue what ye always say.'

'What's that, dear?'

'It's nice t' be nice.'

Chapter 4

SUNDAY IN POGUE'S ENTRY

Jamie and Anna kept the Sabbath. It was a habit with them and the children got it, one after another, as they came along. When the town clock struck twelve on Saturday night, the week's work was done. The customers were given fair warning that at the hour of midnight the bench would be put away until Monday morning. There was nothing theological about the observance. It was a custom, not a code. Anna looked upon it as an over-punctilious notion. More than once she was heard to say: 'The Sabbath was made for maan, Jamie, and not maan for th' Sabbath.'

His answer had brevity and point. 'I don't care a d—n what it was made for, Anna, I'll quit at twelve.' And he quit.

Sometimes Anna would take an unfinished job and finish it herself. There were things in cobbling she could do as well as Jamie. Her defence of doing it in the early hours of the Sabbath was: 'Sure God has more important work to do than to sit up late to watch us mend the boots of the poor, forby it's better to haave ye're boots mended an' go to church than to sit in th' ashes on Sunday an' swallow the smoke of bad turf!'

'Ay,' Jamie would say, 'it's jist wondtherful what ye can do if we haave th' right kind of conscience!'

Jamie's first duty on Sunday was to clean out the

thrush's cage. He was very proud of Dicke, and gave him a bath every morning and a house-cleaning on Sunday. We children loved Sunday. On that day Anna reigned. She wore her little shawl over her shoulders and her hair was enclosed in a newly-tallied white cap. She smoked little, but on Sundays after dinner she always had her 'dhraw' with Jamie. Anna's Sunday chore was to whitewash the hearth-stones and clean the house. When the table was laid for Sunday breakfast and the kettle hung on the chain singing and Anna was in her glory of white linen, the children were supremely happy. In the wildest dreams there was nothing quite as beautiful as that. Whatever hunger, disappointment, or petty quarrel happened during the week, it was forgotten on Sunday. It was a day of supreme peace.

Sunday breakfast was what she called a 'puttiby', something light to tide them over until dinner-time. Dinner was the big meal of the week. At every meal I sat beside my mother. If I had stir-about, I was favoured, but not enough to arouse jealousy: I scraped the pot. If it was 'tay', I got a few bits of the crust of Anna's bread. We called it 'scroof'.

About ten o'clock the preparations for the big dinner began. We had meat once a week. At least it was the plan to have it so often. Of course, there were times when the plan didn't work, but when it did, Sunday was meat day. The word 'meat' was never used. It was 'kitchen' or 'beef'. Both words meant the same thing, and bacon might be meant by either of them.

In nine cases out of ten, Sunday 'kitchen' was a cow's head, a 'calf's head and pluck', a pair of cow's feet, a few sheep's 'trotters', or a quart of sheep's blood. Sometimes it was the entrails of a pig. Only when there was no money for 'kitchen' did we have blood. It was at first fried and then made part of the broth.

The broth-pot on Sunday was the centre. The economic status of a family could be as easily gauged by tasting their broth as by counting the weekly income. Big money, good broth; little money, thin broth. The slimmer the resource the fewer the ingredients. The pot was an index to every condition and the talisman of every family. It was an opportunity to show off. When Jamie donned a 'dickey' once to attend a funeral and came home with it in his pocket, no comment was made; but if Anna made poor broth it was the talk of the entry for a week.

Good broth consisted of 'kitchen', barley, greens, and lithing. Next to 'kitchen' barley was the most expensive ingredient. Folks in Pogue's Entry didn't always have it, but there were a number of cheap substitutes, such as hard peas or horse beans. Amongst half a dozen families in and around the entry there was a broth exchange. Each family made a few extra quarts and exchanged them. They were distributed in quart tin cans. Each can was emptied, washed, refilled, and returned. Ann O'Hare, the chimney-sweep's wife, was usually first on hand. She had the unenviable reputation of being the 'dhirtiest craither' in the community. Jamie called her 'Sooty Ann'.

'There's a gey good smell from yer pot, Anna,' she said; 'what haave ye in it th' day?'

'Oh, jist a few sheep's throtters and a wheen of nettles.'

'Who gethered th' nettles?'

Anna pointed to me.

'Did th' sting bad, me boughal?'

'Deed no, not aany,' I said.

'Did ye squeeze thim tight?'

'I put m' Dah's socks on m' han's.'

'Ah, that's a good thrick.'

Ann had a mouth that looked like a torn pocket. She could pucker it into the queerest shapes. She smacked her thin blue lips, puckered her mouth a number of times while Anna emptied and refilled the can.

'If this is as good as it smells,' she said, as she went out, 'I'll jist sup it myself, and let oul' Billy go chase himself!'

Jamie was the family connoisseur in matters relating to broth. He tasted Ann's. The family waited for the verdict.

'Purty good barley an' lithin',' he said, 'but it smells like Billy's oul' boots.'

'Shame on ye, Jamie,' Anna said.

'Well, give us your high falutin' opinion ov it!'

Anna sipped a spoonful of it and remarked: 'It might be worse.'

'Ay, it's worse where ther's nown, but on yer oath, d'ye think Sooty Ann washed her han's?'

'Good clane dhirt will poison no one, Jamie.'

'Thrue, but this isn't clane dhirt, it's soot—bitther soot!'

It was agreed to pass the O'Hare delectation. When it cooled I quietly gave it to my friend Rover—Mrs Lorimer's dog.

Hen Cassidy came next. Hen's mother was a widow who lived on the edge of want. Hen and I did a little barter and exchange on the side, while Anna emptied and refilled his can. He had scarcely gone when the verdict was rendered:

'Bacon an' nettles,' Jamie said, 'she's as hard up as we are, this week!'

'Poor craither,' Anna said: 'I wondther if she's got aanything besides broth?'

Nobody knew. Anna thought she knew a way to find out.

'Haave ye aany marbles, dear?' she asked me.

'Ay, a wheen.'

'Wud ye give a wheen to me?'

'Ay, are ye goin' t' shoot awhile? If ye are I'll give ye half an' shoot ye fur thim!' I said.

'No, I jist want t' borra some.'

I handed out a handful of marbles.

'Now don't glunch, dear, when I tell ye what I want thim fur.'

I promised.

'Whistle fur Hen,' she said, 'and give him that han'ful of marbles if he'll tell ye what his mother haas fur dinner th' day.'

I whistled and Hen responded.

'I'll bate ye two chanies, Hen, that I know what ye've got fur dinner!'

'I'll bate ye!' said Hen, 'show yer chanies!'

'Show yours!' said I.

Hen had none, but I volunteered to trust him.

'Go on now, guess!' said he.

'Pirtas an' broth!' said I.

'Yer blinked, ye cabbage head, we've got two yards ov thripe forby!'

I carried two quarts to as many neighbours. Mary carried three. As they were settling down to dinner Arthur Gainer arrived with his mother's contribution. Jamie sampled it and laughed outright.

'An' oul' cow put 'er feet in it,' he said. Anna took a taste.

'She didn't keep it in long aither,' was her comment.

'D'ye iver mind seein' barley in Gainer's broth?' Jamie asked.

'I haave no recollection.'

'If there isn't a kink in m' power of remembrance,' Jamie said, 'they've had nothin' but bacon an' nettles since th' big famine.'

'What did th' haave before that?' Anna asked.

'Bacon an' nettles,' he said.

'Did ye ever think, Jamie, how like folks are to th' broth they make?'

'No,' he said, 'but there's no raisin why people should sting jist because they've got nothin' but nettles in their broth!'

The potatoes were emptied out of their pot on the bare table, my father encircling it with his arms to prevent them from rolling off. A little pile of salt was placed beside each person, and each had a big bowl full of broth. The different kinds had lost their identity in the common pot.

In the midst of the meal came visitors.

'Much good may it do ye!' said Billy Baxter, as he walked in with his hands in his pockets.

'Thank ye, Billy, haave a good bowl of broth!'

'Thank ye, thank ye,' he said. 'I don't mind a good bowl ov broth, Anna, but I'd prefer a bowl—jist a bowl of good broth!'

'Ye've had larks for breakvist surely, haaven't ye, Billy?' Anna said.

'No, I didn't, but there's a famine of good broth these days. When I was young we had the rale McKie!'

Billy took a bowl, nevertheless, and went to Jamie's bench to 'sup' it.

Eliza Wallace, the fish woman, came in.

'Much good may it do ye,' she said.

'Thank ye kindly, Liza; sit down an' haave a bowl of broth!'

It was baled out, and Eliza sat down on the floor near the window.

McGrath, the rag man, 'dhrapped in'.

'Much good may it do ye,' he said.

'Thank ye kindly, Tom,' Anna said, 'ye'll surely have a bowl of broth.'

'Jist wan spoonful,' McGrath said.

I emptied my bowl at a nod from Anna, rinsed it out the tub, and filled it with broth. McGrath sat on the doorstep.

After the dinner Anna read a story from the *Weekly Budget,* and the family and guests sat around and listened. Then came the weekly function, over which there invariably arose an altercation amongst the children. It was the Sunday visit of the Methodist tract distributor—Miss Clarke. It was not an unmixed dread, for sometimes she brought a good story and the family enjoyed it. The usual row took place as to who should go to the door and return the tract. It was finally decided that I should face the ordeal. My preparation was to wash my feet, rake my hair into order, and soap it down, cover up a few holes, and await the gentle knock on the door-post. It came, and I bounded to the door, tract in hand.

'Good-afternoon,' she began, 'did your mother read the tract this week?'

'Yis, mem, an' she says it's fine.'

'Do you remember the name of it?'

' "Get yer own Cherries," ' said I.

'*B-u-y*,' came the correction in clear tones from behind the partition.

' "*Buy* yer own Cherries", it is, mem.'

'That's better,' the lady said. 'Some people *get* cherries, other people *buy* them.'

'Ay.'

I never bought any. I knew every wild-cherry tree within twenty miles of Antrim.

The lady saw an opening and went in.

'Did you ever get caught?' she asked.

I hung my head. Then followed a brief lecture on private property—brief, for it was cut short by Anna, who, without any apology or introduction, said, as she confronted the slum evangel: 'Is God our Father?'

'Yes, indeed,' the lady answered.

'An' we are all His childther?'

'Assuredly.'

'Would ye starve yer brother Tom?'

'Of course not.'

'But ye don't mind s' much th' starvation of all yer other wee brothers an' sisters on th' streets, do ye?'

There was a commotion behind the paper partition. The group stood in breathless silence until the hunger question was put, then they 'dunched' each other and made faces. My father took a handful of my hair, and gave it a good-natured but vigorous tug to prevent an explosion.

'Oh, Anna!' she said, 'you are mistaken; I would starve nobody—and far be it from me to accuse——'

'Accuse,' said Anna, raising the gentle voice. 'Why, acushla, nobody needs t' accuse th' poor; th' guilty need no accuser. We're convicted by bein' poor, by bein' born poor an' dying poor, aren't we, now?'

'With the Lord there is neither rich nor poor, Anna.'

'Ay, an' that's no' news to me, but with good folks like you it's different.'

'No, indeed, I assure you I think that exactly.'

'Well, now, if it makes no diff'rence, dear, why do ye come down Pogue's Entry like a bailiff or a process-sarver?'

'I didn't, I just hinted——'

'Ah, ye hinted, an' a wink's as good as a nod to a blind horse. Now tell me truly, an' cross yer heart— wud ye go to Ballycraigie doore an' talk t' wee Willie Chaine as ye talked t' my bhoy jist now?'

'No——'

'No, deed ye wudn't, for th' wudn't let ye, but because we've no choice ye come down here like a petty sessions-magistrate an' make my bhoy feel like a thief because he goes like a crow an' picks a wild cherry or a sloe that wud rot on the tree. D'ye know Luke thirteen an' nineteen?'

The lady opened her Bible, but before she found the passage Anna was reading from her old yellow backless Bible about the birds that lodged in the branches of the trees.

'Did they pay aany rent?' she asked, as she closed the book. 'Did th' foxes have leases fur their holes?'

'No.'

'No, indeed, an' d'ye think He cares less fur boys than birds?'

'Oh, no.'

'Oh, no, an' ye know rightly that everything aroun' Antrim is jist a demesne full o' pheasants an' rabbits for them quality t' shoot, an' we git thransported if we get a male whin we're hungry!'

The lady was tender-hearted and full of sympathy but she hadn't travelled along the same road as Anna and didn't know. Behind the screen the group was jubilant, but when they saw the sympathy on the tract woman's face they sobered and looked sad.

'I must go,' she said, 'and God bless you, Anna.'

And Anna replied, 'God bless you kindly, dear.'

When Anna went behind the screen Jamie grabbed her and pressed her closely to him. 'Ye're a match for John Rae any day, ye are that, woman!'

The kettle was lowered to the burning turf and there was a round of tea. The children and visitors sat on the floor.

'Now that ye're in sich fine fettle, Anna,' Jamie said, 'jist toss th' cups for us!'

She took her own cup, gave it a peculiar twist, and placed it mouth down on the saucer. Then she took it up and examined it quizzically. The leaves straggled hieroglyphically over the inside. The group got their heads together and looked with serious faces at the cup.

'There's a ship comin' across th' sea—an' I see a letther!'

'It's for me, I'll bate,' Jamie said.

'No, dear, it's fur me.'

'Take it,' Jamie said, 'it's maybe a dispossess from oul' Savage th' landlord!'

She took Jamie's cup.

'There's a wee bit of a garden wi' a fence aroun' it.'

'Wud that be Savage givin' us a bit of groun' next year t' raise pirtas?'

'Maybe.'

'Maybe we're goin' t' flit, where there's a perch or two wi' th' house!'

A low whistle outside attracted my attention and I stole quietly away. It was Sonny Johnston, the baker's son, and he had a little bundle under his arm. We boys were discussing a very serious proposition when Anna appeared on the scene.

'Morra, Sonny!'

'Morra, Anna!'

'Aany day but Sunday he may go, dear, but not th' day.'

That was all that was needed. Sonny wanted me to take him bird-nesting. He had the price in the bundle.

'If I give you this *now*,' he said, 'will ye come some other day for nothin'?'

'Ay.'

In the bundle was a 'bap'—a diamond-shaped, flat, penny piece of bread. I rejoined the cup-tossers.

Another whistle. 'That's Arthur,' Anna said.

'No shinny th' day, mind ye.'

I joined Arthur and we sat on the wall of Gainer's pigsty. We hadn't been there long when 'Chisty' McDowell, the superintendent of the Methodist Sunday School, was seen over in Scott's garden rounding up his scholars. We were in his line of vision and he made for us. We saw him coming, and hid in the inner sanctum of the sty. The pig was in the little outer yard. 'Chisty' was a wiry little man of great zeal but little humour. It was his minor talent that came into play on this occasion, however.

'Come, boys, come,' he said, 'I know ye're in there. We've got a beautiful lesson today.'

We crouched in a corner, still silent.

'Come, boys,' he urged, 'don't keep me waiting. The lesson is about the Prodigal Son.'

'Say somethin', Arthur,' I urged.

He did.

'T' h—l wi' the Prodigal Son!' he said, whereupon the little man jumped the low wall into the outer yard and drove the big, grunting, wallowing sow in on top of us! Our yells could be heard a mile away. We came out and were collared and taken off to Sunday School.

When I returned, the cups were all tossed, and the visitors had gone, but Willie Withero had dropped in and was invited to 'stap' for tea. He was our most welcome visitor, and there was but one house where he felt at home.

'Tay' that evening consisted of 'stir-about', Sonny Johnson's unearned bap and buttermilk.

'Willie made more noise "suppin' " his stir-about than Jamie did, and I said: 'Did ye iver hear ov th' cow that got her foot stuck in a bog, Willie?'

'No, boy, what did she do?'

'She got it out!'

A stern look from Jamie prevented the application.

'Tell me, Willie,' Anna said, 'is it thrue that ye can blink a cow so that she can give no milk at all?'

'It's jist a hoax, Anna, some oul' bitch said it an' th' others cackle it from doore to doore. I've naither wife nor wain, chick nor chile, I ate th' bread ov loneliness an' keep m' own company, an' jist bekase I don't blether wi' th' gossoons, th' think I'm un-canny. Isn't that it, Jamie—eh?'

'Ay, ye're right, Willie, it's quare what bletherin' fools there are in this town!'

Willie held his full spoon in front of his mouth while he replied: 'It's you that's the dacent maan, Jamie, 'deed it is.'

'The crocks are empty, dear,' Anna said to me.

After 'tay', to the town well I went for the night's supply of water. When I returned the dishes were washed and on the dresser. The floor was swept and the family were swappin' stories with Withero. Sunday was ever the day of Broth and Romance.

Anna made the best broth and told the best stories. No Sunday was complete without a good story. On the doorstep that night she told one of her best. As she finished, the church bell tolled the curfew. Then the days of the month were tolled off.

'Sammy's arm is gey sthrong th' night,' Willie said.

'Ay,' Jamie said, 'an' th' oul' bell's got a fine ring.'

Chapter 5

HIS ARM IS NOT SHORTENED

When Anna had to choose between love and religion—the religion of an institution—she chose love. Her faith in God remained unshaken, but her methods of approach were the forms of love rather than the symbols or ceremonies of a sect. Twelve times in a quarter of a century she appeared publicly in the parish church. Each time it was to lay on the altar of religion the fruit of her love. Nine-tenths of those twelve congregations would not have known her if they had met her on the street. One-tenth were those who occupied the charity pews.

Religion in our town had arrayed the inhabitants into two hostile camps. She never had any sympathy with the fight. She was neutral. She pointed out to the fanatics around her that the basis of religion was love, and that religion that expressed itself in faction fights must have hate at the bottom of it, not love. She had a philosophy of religion that *worked*. To the sects it would have been rank heresy, but the sects didn't know she existed, and those who were benefited by her quaint and unique application of religion to life were almost as obscure as she was. I was the first to discover her 'heresy' and oppose it. She lived to see me repent of my folly.

In a town of two thousand people less than two hundred were familiar with her face, and half of them knew her because at one time or another they had been to 'Jamie's' to have their shoes made or mended, or because they lived in our immediate vicinity. Of the hundred who knew her face, less than half of them were familiar enough to call her 'Anna'. Of all the people who had lived in Antrim as long as she had, she was the least known.

No feast or function could budge her out of her corner. There came a time when her family became as accustomed to her refusal as she had to her environment and we ceased to coax or urge her. She never attended a picnic, a soiree, or a dance in Antrim. One big opportunity for social intercourse amongst the poor is a wake—she never attended a wake. She often took entire charge of a wake for a neighbour, but she directed the affair from her corner.

She had a slim sort of acquaintance with three intellectual men. They were John Galt, William Green, and John Gordon Holmes, vicars in that order of the parish of Antrim. They visited once a year and at funerals—the funerals of her own dead. None of them knew her. They hadn't time, but there were members of our own family who knew as little of her mind as they did.

She did not seek obscurity. It seemed to have sought and found her. One avenue of escape after another was closed, and she settled down at last to her lot in the chimney-corner. Her hopes, beliefs, and aspirations were expressed in what she did rather than in what she said, though she said much, much that is still treasured, long after she has passed away.

Henry Lecky was a young fisherman on Lough Neagh. He was a great favourite with the children of the entries. He loved to bring us a small trout each when he returned after a long fishing trip. He died suddenly, and Eliza, his mother, came at once for help to the chimney-corner.

'He's gone, Anna, he's gone!' she said, as she dropped on the floor beside Anna.

'An' ye want me t' do fer yer dead what ye'd do for mine, 'Liza?'

'Ay, ay, Anna, yer God's angel to yer frien's.'

'Go an fetch 'Liza Conlon, Jane Burrows, and Marget Houston!' was Anna's order to Jamie.

The women came at once. The plan was outlined, the labour apportioned, and they went to work. Jamie went for the carpenter and hired William Gainer to dig the grave. Eliza Conlon made the shroud, Jane Burrows and Anna washed and laid out the corpse, and Mrs Houston kept Eliza in Anna's bed until the preliminaries for the wake were completed.

'Ye can go now, Mrs Houston,' Anna said, 'an' I'll mind 'Liza.'

'The light's gone out o' m' home, an' darkness fills m' heart, Anna, an' it's the sun that'll shine for m' no more! Ochone, ochone!'

"'Liza, dear, I've been where ye are now, too often not t' know that aanything that aanybody says is jist like spittin' at a burnin' house t' put it out. Yer boy's gone—we can't bring 'im back. Fate's cut yer heart in two, an' oul Docther Time an' the care of God are about the only shure cures goin'.'

'Cudn't the ministher help a little if he was here, Anna?'

'If ye think so, I'll get him, 'Liza!'

'He might put th' love of God in me!'

'Puttin' th' love of God in ye isn't like stuffin' yer mouth with a pirta, 'Liza!'

'That's so, it is, but he might thry, Anna!'

'Well, ye'll haave 'im.'

Mr Green came and gave 'Liza what consolation he could. He read the appropriate prayer, repeated the customary words. He did it all in a tender tone and departed.

'Ye feel fine afther that, don't ye, 'Liza?'

'Ay, but Henry's dead, an' will no come back!'

'Did ye expect Mr Green t' bring 'im?'

'No.'

'What did ye expect, 'Liza?'

'I dunno.'

'Shure ye don't. Ye didn't expect aanything, an' ye got just what ye expected. Ah, wuman, God isn't a printed book t' be carried aroun' by' a man in fine clothes, nor a gold cross t' be danglin' at the watch chain ov a priest.'

'What is He, Anna, yer wiser nor me; tell a poor craither in throuble, do?'

'If ye'll lie very quiet, 'Liza—jist cross yer hands and listen—if ye do, I'll thry!'

'Ay, bless ye, I'll blirt no more; go on!'

'Wee Henry is over there in his shroud, isn't he?'

'Ay, God rest his soul.'

'He'll rest Henry's, 'Liza, but He'll haave the divil's own job wi' yours if ye don't help 'im.'

'Och, ay, thin I'll be at pace.'

'As I was sayin', Henry's body is jist as it was yesterday, han's, legs, heart, an' head, aren't they?'

'Ay, 'cept cold and stiff.'

'What's missing, then?'

'His blessed soul, God love it.'

'That's right. Now, when the spirit laves th' body we say th' body's dead, but it's jist a partnership gone broke, wan goes up an' wan goes down. I've

67

always thot that kissin' a corpse was like kissin' a cage whin the bird's dead—*there's nothin' in it*. Now answer me this, 'Liza Lecky. Is Henry a livin' spirit or a dead body?'

'A livin' spirit, God prosper it.'

'Ay, an' God is th' same kind, but Henry's can be at but wan point at once, while God's is everywhere at once. He's so big He can cover the world, an' so small He can get in be a crack in th' glass or a kayhole.'

'I've got four panes broke, Anna!'

'Well, they're jist like four doores.'

'Feeries can come in that way, too.'

'Ay, but feeries can't sew up a broken heart, acushla.'

'Where's Henry's soul, Anna?' Eliza asked, as if the said soul was a navvy over whom Anna stood as gaffer.

'It may be here at yer bedhead now, but yer more in need of knowin' where God's Spirit is, 'Liza.'

Jamie entered with a cup of tea.

'For a throubled heart,' he said, 'there's nothin' in this world like a rale good cup o' tay.'

'God bless ye kindly, Jamie, I've a sore heart, an' I'm as dhry as a whistle.'

'Now, Jamie, put th' cups down on th' bed,' Anna said, 'an' then get out, like a good bhoy!'

'I want a crack wi' Anna, Jamie,' Eliza said.

'Well, ye'll go farther an' fare worse—she's a buffer at that!'

Eliza sat up in bed while she drank the tea. When she drained her cup she handed it over to Anna.

'Toss it, Anna, maybe there's good luck in it fur me.'

'No, dear, it's a hoax at best; jist now it wud be

pure blasphemy. Ye don't need luck, ye need at this minute th' help of God.'

'Och, ay, ye're right; jist talk t' me ov Him.'

'I was talkin' about His Spirit when Jamie came in.'

'Ay.'

'It comes in as many ways as there's need fur its comin', and that's quite a wheen.'

'God knows.'

'Ye'll haave t' be calm, dear, before He'd come t' ye in aany way.'

'Ay, but I'm at pace now, Anna, amn't I?'

'Well, now, get out here an' get down on th' floor on yer bare knees and haave a talk wi 'Im.'

Eliza obeyed implicitly. Anna knelt beside her.

'I don't know what t' say.'

'Say afther me,' and Anna told of an empty home and a sore heart. When she paused, Eliza groaned.

'Now tell 'Im to lay 'Is hand on yer tired head in token that He's wi' ye in yer disthress!'

Even to a dull intellect like Eliza's the suggestion was startling.

'Wud He do it, Anna?'

'Well, jist ask 'Im an' then wait an' see!'

In faltering tones Eliza made her request and waited. As gently as falls an autumn leaf Anna laid her hand on Eliza's head, held it there for a moment and removed it.

'Oh, oh, oh, He's done it, Anna, He's done it, glory be t' God, He's done it!'

'Rise up, dear,' Anna said, 'an' tell me about it.'

'There was a nice feelin' went down through me, Anna, an' th' han' was jist like yours!'

'The han' was mine, but it was God's too.' Anna wiped her spectacles and took Eliza over close to the window while she read a text of the Bible. 'Listen, dear,' Anna said, ' "God's arm is not shortened." Did ye think that an arm could be stretched from beyont th' clouds t' Pogue's Entry?'

'Ay.'

'No, dear, but God takes a han' wherever He can find it, and jist diz what He likes wi' it. Sometimes He takes a bishop's and lays it on a child's head in benediction, then He takes the han' of a docther t' relieve pain, th' han' of a mother t' guide her chile, an' sometimes He takes th' han' of an aul' craither like me t' give a bit of comfort to a neighbour. But they're all han's touch't be His Spirit, an' His Spirit is everywhere lukin' for han's to use.'

Eliza looked at her open-mouthed for a moment.

'Tell me, Anna,' she said, as she put her hands on her shoulders, 'was th' han' that bro't home trouts fur th' childther God's han' too?'

'Ay, 'deed it was.'

'Oh, glory be t' God—thin I'm at pace—isn't it gran' t' think on—isn't it now?'

Eliza Conlon abruptly terminated the conversation by announcing that all was ready for the wake.

'Ah, but it's the purty corpse he is,' she said, '—luks jist like life!'

The three women went over to the Lecky home. It was a one-room place. The big bed stood in the corner. The corpse was 'laid-out' with the hands clasped.

The moment Eliza entered she rushed to the bed and fell on her knees beside it. She was quiet, however, and after a moment's pause she raised her head and laying a hand on the folded hands, said: 'Ah, han's ov God t' be so cold an' still!'

Anna stood beside her until she thought she had

70

stayed long enough, then led her gently away. From that moment Anna directed the wake and the funeral from her chimney-corner.

'Here's a basket ov flowers for Henry, Anna, the childther gethered thim th' day,' Maggie McKinstry said, as she laid them down on the hearthstones beside Anna.

'Ye've got some time, Maggie?'

'Oh, ay.'

'Make a chain ov them an' let it go all th' way aroun' th' body, they'll look purty that way, don't ye think so?'

'Illigant, indeed, to be shure! 'Deed I'll do it.' And it was done.

To Eliza Conlon was given the task of providing refreshments. I say 'task', for after the carpenter was paid for the coffin and Jamie Scott for the hearse there was only six shillings left.

'Get whey for th' childther,' Anna said, and 'childther' in this catalogue ran up into the twenties.

For the older 'childther' there was something from Mrs Lorimer's public-house—something that was kept under cover and passed around late, and later still diluted and passed around again. Concerning this item Anna said: 'Wather it well, dear, an' save in their wits; they've got little enough now, God save us all!'

'Anna,' said Sam Johnston, 'I am told you have charge of Henry's wake. Is there anything I can do?'

Sam was the tall, imperious precentor of the Mill Row meeting house. He was also the chief baker of the town, and 'looked up to' in matters relating to morals as well as loaves.

'Mister Gwynn has promised t' read a chapther, Mister Johnston. He'll read, maybe, the fourteenth of John. If he diz, tell him t' go aisy over th' twelfth verse an' explain that th' works He did can be done in Antrim by any poor craither who's got th' Spirit.'

Sam straightened up to his full height and in measured words said: 'Ye know, no doubt, Anna, that Misther Gwynn is a Churchman an' I'm a Presbyterian. He wouldn't take kindly to a hint from a Mill Row maan, I fear, especially on a disputed text.'

'Well, dear knows if there's aanything this oul' world needs more than another, it's an undisputed text. Couldn't ye find us wan, Misther Johnston?'

'All texts are disputed,' he said, 'but there are texts not in dispute.'

'I think I could name wan at laste, Misther Johnson.'

'Maybe.'

''Deed, no maybe at all, but *surebe*. Jamie, dear, get m' th' Bible, if ye plaze.'

While Jamie got the Bible she wiped her glasses and complained in a gentle voice about the 'mortal pity of it' that texts were pins for Christians to stick in each other's flesh.

'Here it is,' she said, ' "Th' poor ye haave always with ye." '

'Ay,' Sam said, 'an' how true it is.'

''Deed it's true, but who did He mane by "ye"?'

'Th' world, I suppose.'

'Not all th' world, by a spoonful, but a wheen of thim like Sandy Somerville, who's got a signboard in front of his back that tells he ates too much while the rest of us haave backbones that could as aisily be felt before as behine!'

'So that's what you call an *undisputed* text?'

She looked over the rim of her spectacles at him

for a moment in silence, and then said slowly: 'Ochone—w-e-l-l—tell Mister Gwynn t' read what he likes, it'll mane th' same aanyway.'

Kitty Coyle came in. Henry and she were engaged. They had known each other since childhood. Her eyes were red with weeping. Henry's mother led her by the arm.

'Anna, dear,' Eliza said, 'she needs ye as much as me. Give 'er a bit ov comfort.'

They went into the little bedroom and the door was shut. Jamie stood as sentry.

When they came out young Johnny Murdock, Henry's chum, was sitting on Jamie's workbench.

'I want ye t' take good care of Kitty th' night, Johnny. Keep close t' 'er, and when th' moon comes out take 'er down the garden t' get fresh air. It'll be stuffy wi' all th' people an' the corpse in Lecky's.'

'Ay,' he said, 'I'll do all I can.'

To Kitty she said, 'I've asked Johnny t' keep gey close t' ye till it's all over, Kitty. Ye'll understand.'

'Ay,' Kitty said, 'Henry loved 'im more'n aany maan on th' Lough!'

'Had tay yit?' Willie Withero asked, as he blundered in on the scene.

'No, Willie, 'deed we haaven't thought ov it!'

'Well, t' haave yer bowels think yer throat's cut isn't saucy!' he said.

The fire was low and the kettle cold.

'Here, Johnny,' Withero said, 'jist run over t' Farren's for a ha'porth ov turf an' we'll haave a cup of tay fur these folks who're workin' overtime palaverin' about th' dead! Moses alive, wan corpse is enough fur a week or two—don't kill us all entirely!'

Shortly after midnight Anna went over to see how things were at the wake. They told her of the singing

73

of the children, of the beautiful chapther by Misther Gwynn, and the 'feelin'' prayer by Graham Shannon. The whey was sufficient and nearly everybody had 'a dhrap o' th' craither' and a bite of fadge.

'Ah, Anna dear,' Eliza said, 'shure it's yerself that knows how t' make a moi'ty go th' longest distance over dhry throats an' empty stomachs! 'Deed it was a revival an' a faste in wan, an' th' only pity is that poor Henry cudn't enjoy it!'

The candles were burned low in the sconces, the flowers around the corpse had faded, a few tongues, loosened by stimulation, were still wagging, but the laughter had died down and the stories were all told. There had been a hair-raising ghost story that had sent a dozen home before the *respectable* time of departure. The empty stools had been carried outside and were largely occupied by lovers.

Anna drew Eliza's head to her breast, and pressing it gently to her, said, 'I'm proud of ye, dear, ye've borne up bravely! Now I'm goin' t' haave a few winks in th' corner, for there'll be much to do the morra.'

Scarcely had the words died on her lips when Kitty Coyle gave vent to a scream of terror that brought the mourners to the door and terrified those outside.

'What ails ye, in the name of God?' Anna said.

She was too terrified to speak at once. The mourners crowded closely together.

'Watch!' Kitty said, as she pointed with her finger toward Conlon's pigsty. Johnny Murdock had his arm around Kitty's waist to keep her steady and assure her of protection. They watched and waited. It was a bright moonlight night, and save for the deep shadows of the houses and hedges, as clear as day. Tensely nerve-stung, open-mouthed, and wild-eyed, stood the group, for what seemed to them hours. In a

few minutes a white figure was seen emerging from the pigsty. The watchers were transfixed in terror. Most of them clutched at each other nervously. Old Mrs Houston the midwife, who had told the ghost story at the wake, dropped in a heap. Peter Hannen and Jamie Wilson carried her indoors.

The white figure stood on the pathway leading through the gardens for a moment, and then returned to the sty. Most of the watchers fled to their homes. Some didn't move, because they had lost the power to do so. Others just stood.

'It's a hoax an' a joke,' Anna said. 'Now wan of you men go down there an' see!'

No one moved. Every eye was fixed on the pigsty. A long-drawn-out, mournful cry was heard. It was all that tradition had described as the cry of the Banshee.

'The Banshee it is! Ah, merciful God, which ov us is t' b' tuk, I wondher?' It was Eliza who spoke, and she continued, directing her talk to Anna, 'An' it's th' long arm ov th' Almighty it is raychin' down t' give us warnin', don't ye think so now, Anna?'

'If it's wan arm of God, I know where th' other is, 'Liza!' Addressing the terror-stricken watchers, Anna said: 'Stand here, don't budge, wan of ye!'

Along the sides of the houses in the deep shadow Anna walked until she got to the end of the row; just around the corner stood the sty. In the shadow she stood with her back to the wall and waited. The watchers were breathless and what they saw a minute later gave them a syncope of the heart that they never forgot. They saw the white figure emerge again and they saw Anna stealthily approach and enter into what they thought was a struggle with it. They gasped when they saw her a moment later bring the white figure along with her. As she came nearer it looked limp and pliable, for it hung over her arm.

'It's that divil, Ben Green!' she said, as she threw a white sheet at her feet.

'Hell roast 'im on a brandther!' said one.

'The divil gut 'im like a herrin'! said another.

Four of the younger men, having been shamed by their own cowardice, made a raid on the sty, and next day when Ben came to the funeral he looked very much the worse for wear.

Ben was a friend of Henry's and a good deal of a practical joker. Anna heard of what happened, and she directed that he be one of the four men to lower the coffin into the grave, as a moiety of consolation. Johnny Murdock made strenuous objections to this.

'Why?' Anna asked.

'Bekase,' he said, 'shure th' divil nearly kilt Kitty be th' fright.'

'But she was purty comfortable th' rest of th' time?'

'Oh, ay.'

'Ye lifted a gey big burden from 'er heart last night, didn't ye, Johnny?'

'Ay; an' if ye won't let on, I'll tell ye, Anna.' He came close and whispered into her ear: 'Am goin' t' thry danged hard t' take th' heart as well as th' throuble!'

'What diz Kitty think?'

'She's switherin'.'

Chapter 6

THE APOTHEOSIS OF HUGHIE THORNTON

Anna was an epistle to Pogue's Entry, and my only excuse for dragging Hughie Thornton into this narrative is that he was a commentary on Anna. He was only once in our house, but that was an 'occasion', and for many years we dated things that happened about that time as 'about', 'before', or 'after' 'the night Hughie stayed in the pigsty.'

We lived in the social cellar; Hughie led a precarious existence in the *sub-cellar*. He was the beggarman of several towns, of which Antrim was the largest. He was a short, thick-set man with a pock-marked face, eyes like a mouse, eyebrows that looked like well-worn scrubbing brushes, and a beard cropped close with scissors or a knife. He wore two coats, two pairs of trousers, and several waistcoats—all at the same time, winter and summer. His old battered hat looked like a crow's nest. His wardrobe was so elaborately patched that practically nothing at all of the originals remained; even then patches of his old, withered skin could be seen at various angles. The thing that attracted my attention more than anything else about him was his pockets. He had dozens of them, and they were always full of bread crusts, scraps of meat, and cooking utensils, for like a snail he carried his domicile on his back. His boots looked as if a blacksmith had made them, and for whangs (laces) he used strong wire.

He was pre-eminently a citizen of the world. He had not lived in a house in half a century. A haystack in summer, and a pigsty in winter sufficed him. He had a deep gramophone voice, and when he spoke the sound was like the creaking of a barn door on rusty hinges. When he came to town he was to us what a circus is to boys of more highly favoured communities. There were several interpretations of Hughie. One was that he was a 'sent back'. That is, he had gone to the gates of a less cumbersome life and Peter or the porter at the other gate had sent him back to perform some unfulfilled task. Another was that he was a nobleman of an ancient line who was wandering over the earth in disguise in search of the Grail. A third, and the most popular one, was that he was just a common beggar, and an unmitigated liar. The second interpretation was made more plausible by the fact that he rather enjoyed his reputation as a liar, for wise ones said: 'He's jist lettin' on.'

On one of his semi-annual visits to Antrim, Hughie got into a barrel of trouble. He was charged—rumour charged him—with having blinked a widow's cow. It was noised abroad that he had been caught in the act of 'skellyin' ' at her. The story gathered in volume as it went from mouth to mouth, until it crystallised as a crime in the minds of half a dozen of our toughest citizens—boys who hankered for excitement as a hungry stomach hankers for food. He was finallly rounded up in a field adjoining the Mill Row meeting-house and pelted with stones. I was of the 'gallery' that watched the fun. I watched until a track of blood streaked down Hughie's pock-marked face. Then I ran home and told Anna.

'Ma!' I yelled breathlessly, 'they're killin' Hughie Thornton!'

Jamie threw his work down and accompanied Anna over the little garden patches to the wall that protected the field. Through the gap they went, and found poor Hughie in bad shape. He was crying and he cried like a brass band. His head and face had been cut in several places, and his face and clothes were red.

They brought him home. A crowd followed and filled Pogue's Entry, a crowd that was about equally divided in sentiment against Hughie and against the toughs.

I borrowed a can of water from Mrs McGrath and another from the Gainers, and Anna washed old Hughie's wounds in Jamie's tub. It was a great operation. Hughie, of course, refused to divest himself of any clothing, and as she said afterwards, it was like 'dhressin' th' wounds of a haystack'.

One of my older brothers came home and cleared the entry, and we sat down to our stir-about and buttermilk. An extra cup of good hot strong tea was the finishing touch to the Samaritan act. Jamie had scant sympathy with the beggar-man. He had always called him hard names in language not lawful to utter, and even in this critical exigency was not over tender. Anna saw a human need, and tried to supply it.

'Did ye blink th' cow?' Jamie asked, as we sat around the candle after supper.

'Divil a blink,' said Hughie.

'What did th' raise a hue-an'-cry fur?' was the next question.

'I was fixin' m' galluses over Crawford's hedge, whin a gomeral luked over an' says, says he: 'Morra, Hughie!'

' "Morra, bhoy!" says I.

' "Luks like snow," says he (it was in July).

' "Ay," says I, "we're goin' t' haave more weather; th' sky's in a bad art" ' (direction).

Anna arose, put her little Sunday shawl around her shoulders, tightened the strings of her cap under her chin, and went out. We gasped with astonishment! What on earth could she be going out for? She never went out at night. Everybody came to her. There was something so mysterious in that sudden exit that we just looked at our guest without understanding a word he said.

Jamie opened up another line of inquiry.

'Th' say yer a terrible liar, Hughie.'

'I am that,' Hughie said, without the slightest hesitation. 'I'm th' champ'yun liar ov County Anthrim.'

'How did ye get th' belt?'

'Aisy, as aisy as tellin' the thruth.'

'That's harder nor ye think.'

'So's lyin', Jamie!'

'Tell us how ye won th' champ'yunship.'

'Whin I finish this dhraw.'

He took a live coal and stoked up the bowl of his old cutty-pipe. The smacking of his lips could have been heard at the mouth of Pogue's Entry. We waited with breathless interest. When he had finished he knocked the ashes out on the toe of his brogue and talked for nearly an hour of the great event in which he covered himself with glory.

It was a fierce encounter, according to Hughie, the then Champion being a Ballymena man by the name of Jack Rooney. Jack and a bunch of vagabonds sat on a stone-pile near Ballyclare when Hughie hove in sight. The beggar-man was at once challenged to divest himself of half his clothes or enter the contest. He entered, with the result that Ballymena lost the championship! The concluding round, as Hughie recited it, was as follows:

'I dhruv a nail throo th' moon wanst,' said Jack.

'Ye did, did ye,' said Hughie, 'but did ye iver hear ov the maan that climbed up over the clouds wid a hammer in his hand an' clinched it on th' other side?'

'No,' said the champion.

'I'm him!' said Hughie.

'I'm bate!' said Jack Rooney, 'an' begods if I wor St Peether I'd kape ye outside th' gate till ye tuk it out again!'

Anna returned with a blanket rolled up under her arm. She gave Hughie his choice between sleeping in Jamie's corner among the lasts or occupying the pigsty. He chose the pigsty, but before he retired I begged Anna to ask him about the Banshee.

'Did ye ever really see a Banshee, Hughie?'

'Is there aanythin' a champ'yun liar haasn't seen?' Jamie interrupted.

'Ay,' Hughie said, ' 'deed there is, he nivir seen a maan who'd believe 'im, even whin he was tellin' the thruth!'

'That's broth for your noggin', Jamie,' Anna said.

Encouraged by Anna, Hughie came back with a thrust that increased Jamie's sympathy for him.

'I'm undther yer roof an' beholdin' t' yer kindness, but I'd like t' ax ye a civil quest'yun if I may be so bowld.'

'Ay, go on.'

'Did ye blow a farmer's brains out in th' famine fur a pint ov milk?'

'It's a lie!' Jamie said indignantly.

'Well, me bhoy, there must b' quite a wheen thrainin' fur me belt in Anthrim!'

'There's something in that, Hughie!'

'Ay, somethin' Hughie Thornton didn't put in it!'

We youngsters were irritated and impatient over what seemed to us useless palaver about minor details. We wanted the story and wanted it at once, for we understood that Hughie went to bed with the crows, and we stood in terror lest this huge bundle of pockets, with its unearthly voice, should vanish into thin air.

'D'ye know McShane?' he asked.

'Ay, middlin'.'

'Ax 'im what Hughie Thornton towld 'im wan night be th' hour ov midnight an' afther. Ax 'im, I say, an' he'll swear be th' Holy Virgin an' St Peether t' it!'

'Jist tell us aanyway, Hughie,' Anna urged, and the beggar-man proceeded.

'I was be th' oul' Quaker graveyard be Moylena wan night whin th' shadows fell, an' bein' more tired than most, I slipt in an' lay down be th' big wall t' slape. I cros't m'self seven times, an' says I, "God rest th' sowls ov all here, an' God prosper th' sowl ov Hughie Thornton." I wint t' slape, an slept th' slape of th' just till twelve be th' clock. I was shuk out ov slape by a screech that waked th' dead!

'Och, be th' powers, Jamie, me hair stud like the brisels on O'Hara's hog. I lukt and what m' eyes lukt upon froze me blood like icicles hingin' frum th' thatch. It was a woman in a white shift, young and beautiful, wid her hair stramin' down her back. She sat on th' wall wid her head in her han's keenin' an' moanin': "Ochone, ochone!" I thried to spake, but m' tongue cluv t' th' roof ov m' mouth. I tried t' move a han' but it wudn't budge. M' legs an' feet wor as stiff and shtrait as th' legs ov thim tongs in yer

83

chimley. Och, but it's th' prackus I was from top t' toe! Dead intirely was I but fur th' eyes an' th' wit behint thim. She ariz an' walked up an' down, back an' fort', up an' down, back an' fort', keenin' an' cryin' an' wringin' her han's! Man alive, didn't she carry on terrible! Purty soon wid a yell she lept into the graveyard, thin she lept on th' wall, thin I heerd her on th' road, keenin'; an' iverywhere she wint wor long bars of light like sunbames streamin' throo th' holes in a barn. Th' keenin become waker an' waker till it died down like the cheep ov a willy-wag-tail far off be the ind ov th' road.

'I got up an' ran like the red shank t' McShane's house. I dundthered at his doore till he opened it, thin I towld him I'd seen th' Banshee!

' "That bates Bannagher!" says he.

' "It bates th' divil," says I. "But whose fur above th' night is what I'd like t' know?"

' "Oul' Misther Chaine,' says he, "as sure as gun's iron!" '

The narrative stopped abruptly, stopped at McShane's door.

'Did oul' Misther Chaine die that night?' Anna asked.

'Ax McShane!' was all the answer he gave, and we were sent off to bed.

Hughie was escorted to the pigsty with his blanket and candle. What Jamie saw on the way to the pigsty made the perspiration stand in big beads on his furrowed brow. Silhouetted against the sky were several figures. Some were within a dozen yards, others were farther away. Two sat on a low wall that divided the Adair and Mulholland gardens. They were silent and motionless, but there was no mistake about it. He directed Anna's attention to them and she made light of it. When they returned to the house Jamie expressed fear for the life of the beggar-man. Anna whispered something into his ear, for she knew that we were wide awake. They went into their room conversing in an undertone.

The thing was so uncanny to me that it was three o'clock next morning before I went to sleep. As early as six there was an unusual shuffling and clattering of feet over the cobblestones in Pogue's Entry. We knew everybody in the entry by the sound of their footfall. The clatter was by the feet of strangers.

I 'dunched' my brother, who lay beside me, with my elbow.

'Go an' see if oul' Hughie's livin' or dead,' I said.

'Ye cudn't kill 'im,' he said.

'How d'ye know?'

'I heerd a quare story about 'im last night!'

'Where?'

'In th' barber's shop.'

'Is he a feerie?'

'No.'

'What is he?'

'Close yer trap an' lie still!'

Somebody opened the door and walked in. I slid into my clothes and climbed down. It was Withero. He shook Anna and Jamie in their bed, and asked in a loud voice: 'What's all this palaver about an oul' trollop what niver earned salt t' 'is pirtas?'

'Go on t' yer stone-pile, Willie,' Anna said, as she sat up in bed; 'what ye don't know will save docther's bills.'

'If I catch m'self thinkin' aanythin' saucy ov that aul' haythen baste I'll change m' name!' he said, as he turned and left in high dudgeon.

When I got to the pigsty there were several early

85

callers lounging around. 'Jowler' Hainey sat on a big stone near the slit. Mary McConnaughy stood with her arms akimbo, within a yard of the door, and Tommy Wilson was peeping into the sty through a knot-hole on the side. I took my turn at the hole. Hughie had evidently been awakened early. He was sitting arranging his pockets. Con Mulholland came down the entry with his gun over his shoulder. He had just returned from his vigil as night watchman at the Greens, and was going the longest way around to his home.

He leaned his gun against the house side and lit his pipe. Then he opened the sty door, softly, and said: 'Morra, Hughie.'

'Morra, Con,' came the answer, in calliope tones from our guest.

'Haave ye a good stock ov tubacco?' Con asked Hughie.

'I cud shtart a pipe shap, Con, fur be th' first trake ov dawn I found five new pipes an' five half ounces ov tubacca inside th' door ov th' sty!'

'Take this bit too. Avic, ye don't come often,' and he gave him a small package and took his departure.

Eliza Conlon brought a cup of tea. Without even looking in, she pushed the little door ajar, laid it just inside, and went away without a word. Mulholland and Hainey seemed supremely concerned about the weather. From all they said it was quite evident that each of them had 'jist dhrapped aroun' t' find out what Jamie thought ov th' prospects fur a fine day!' Old Sandy Somerville came hatless and in his shirt-sleeves, his hands deep in his pockets and his big watch-chain dangling across what Anna called the 'front of his back'. Sandy was some quality, too, and owned three houses.

'Did aany o' ye see my big orange cat?' he asked the callers.

Without waiting for an answer he opened the door of the pigsty and peeped in.

By the time Hughie scrambled out there were a dozen men, women, and boys around the sty. As the beggar-man struggled up through his freight to his feet, the eyes of the crowd were scrutinising him. Sandy shook hands with him and wished him a pleasant journey.

Hainey hoped he would live long and prosper. As he expressed the hope, he furtively stuffed into one of Hughie's pockets a small package.

Anna came out and led Hughie into the house for breakfast. The little crowd moved toward the door. On the doorstep she turned around and said: 'Hughie's goin' t' haave a cup an' a slice, an' go. Ye can all see him in a few minutes. Excuse me if I shut the doore, but Jamie's givin' the thrush its mornin' bath, an' it might fly out.'

She gently closed the door, and we were again alone with the guest.

'The luck ov God is m' portion here,' he said, looking at Anna.

Nothing was more evident. His pockets were taxed to their full capacity, and those who gathered around the table that morning wished that the 'luck of God' would spread a little.

'Th' feeries must haave been t' see ye,' Jamie said, eyeing his pockets.

'Ay, gey sauncy feeries, too!'

'Did ye see aany, Hughie?' Anna asked.

'No, but I had a wondtherful dhrame.'

The announcement was a disappointment to us. We had dreams of our own and to have right at our fireside the one man in all the world who *saw* things and get merely a dream from him was, to say the least, discouraging.

'I thocht I heer'd th' rat, tap; rat, tap, of th' Lepracaun—th' feerie shoemaker.

' "Is that th' Lepracaun?" says I. "If it is I want m' three wishes."

' "Git thim out," says he, "fur I'm gey busy th' night."

'Sound slape th' night an' safe journey th' morra," says I.

' "Get your third out or I'm gone," says he.

'I scratched m' head an' swithered, but divil a third cud I think ov. Jist as he was goin', "Oh," says I, "I want a pig fur this sty!"

' "Ye'll git him!" sayd he, an' off he wint.'

Here was something, after all, that gave us more excitement than a Banshee story. We had a sty. We had hoped for years for a pig. We had been forced often to use some of the sty for fuel, but in good time Jamie had always replaced the boards. This was a real vision, and we were satisfied. Jamie's faith in Hughie soared high at the time, but a few months later it fell to zero. Anna, with a twinkle in her eye, would remind us of Hughie's prophecy. One day he would wipe the vision oft the slate.

'T' h—l wi' Hughie!' he said. 'Some night he'll come back an' slape there, thin we'll have a pig in th' sty shure!'

As he left our house that morning he was greeted in a most unusual manner by a score of people who crowded the entry. Men and women gathered around him. They inspected the wounds. They gave their blessings in as many varieties as there were people present. The new attitude towards the beggar baffled us. Generally he was considered a good deal of a nuisance and something of a fraud, but that morning he was looked upon as a saint—as one inspired, as one capable of bestowing benedictions on the young and giving 'luck' to the old. Out of their penury and want they brought gifts of food, tobacco, cloth for patches, and needles and thread. He was overwhelmed and overburdened, and as his mission of gathering food for a few weeks was accomplished he made for the town head when he left the entry.

The small crowd grew into a big one, and he was the centre of a throng as he made his way north. When he reached the town well, Maggie McKinstry had several small children in waiting, and Hughie was asked to give them a blessing. It was a new atmosphere to him, but he bungled through it. The more unintelligible his jabbering, the more assured were the recipients of his power to bless. One of the boys who stoned him was brought by his father to ask forgiveness.

'God save ye kindly,' Hughie said to him. 'Th' woonds ye made haave been turned into blessin's galore!'

He came in despised. He went out a saint.

It proved to be Hughie's last visit to Antrim. His going out of life was a mystery, and as the years went by tradition accorded him an exit not unlike that of Moses. I was amongst those the current of whose lives were supposed to have been changed by the touch of his hand on that last visit. Anna alone knew the secret of his alleged sainthood. She was the author and publisher of it. That night when she left us with Hughie she gathered together in 'Liza Conlon's a few 'hand-picked' people whose minds were as an open book to her. She told them that the beggarman was of an ancient line, wandering the earth in search of the Holy Grail, but that as he wandered he was recording in a secret book the deeds of the poor. She knew exactly how the news would travel and where. One superstition stoned him and another canonised him.

'Dear,' she said to me, many, many years afterwards, 'a good thought will travel as fast an' as far as a bad wan if it gets th' right start!'

Chapter 7

IN THE GLOW OF A PEAT FIRE

'It's a quare world,' Jamie said one night, as we sat in the glow of a peat fire.

'Ay, 'deed yer right, Jamie,' Anna replied, as she gazed into the smokeless flames.

He took his short, black pipe out of his mouth, spat into the burning sods, and added: 'I wondther if it's as quare t' everybody, Anna.'

'Ochance,' she replied, 'it's quare t' poor craithers who haave naither mate, money, nor marbles, nor chalk t' make th' ring.'

There had been but one job that day—a pair of McGuckin's boots. They had been half-soled and heeled, and my sister had taken them home, with orders what to bring home for supper.

The last handful of peat had been put on the fire. The cobbler's bench had been put aside for the night and we gathered closely round the hearth.

The town clock struck eight.   'What th' h—l's kapin' th' hussy!' Jamie said petulantly.

'Hugh's at a Fenian meeting more'n likely, an' it's worth a black eye for th' wife t' handle money when he's gone,' Anna suggested.

'More likely he's sleepin' off a dhrunk,' he said.

'No, Jamie, he laves that t' craithers who give 'im a livin'.'

'Yer no judge o' human naiture, Anna. A squint out o' th' tail o' yer eye at what McGuckin carries in

91

front ov 'im wud tell ye betther if ye had th' wits to observe.'

Over the fire hung a pot on the chain, and close to the turf coals sat the kettle, singing. Nothing of that far-off life has left a more lasting impression than the singing of the kettle. It sang a dirge that night, but it usually sang of hope. It was ever the harbinger of the thing that was most indispensable in that home of want—a cup of tea. Often it was tea without milk, sometimes without sugar, but always tea. If it came to a choice between tea and bread, we went without bread.

Anna did not relish the reflection on her judgement, and remained silent.

There was a loud noise at the door.

'Jazus!' Jamie exclaimed, 'it's snowin'.'

Someone was kicking the snow off against the door-post. The latch was lifted, and in walked Felix Boyle, the bogman.

'What th' blazes are ye in th' dark fur?' Felix asked in a deep, hoarse voice. His old rabbit-skin cap was pulled down over his ears, his head and shoulders were covered with snow. As he shook it off we shivered. We were in debt to Felix for a load of turf, and we suspected he had called for the money. Anna lit the candle she was saving for supper-time. The bogman threw his cap and overcoat over in the corner on the lasts, and sat down. 'I'm frozen t' death!' he said, as he proceeded to take off his brogues.

As he came up close to the coals, we were smitten with his foul breath, and in consequence gave him a wider berth. He had been drinking.

'Where's the mare?' Anna asked.

'Gone home, th' bitch o' h—l,' he said, 'an' she's

92

got m' load o' turf wid 'er, bad cess t' 'er dhirty sowl!'

The town clock struck nine.

Felix removed his socks, pushed his stool aside, and sat down on the mud floor. A few minutes later he was flat on his back, fast asleep and snoring loudly.

The fire grew smaller. Anna husbanded the diminishing embers by keeping them closely together with the long tongs. The wind howled and screamed. The window rattled, the door creaked on its hinges, and every few minutes a gust of wind came down the chimney and blew the ashes into our faces. We huddled nearer the fire.

'Can't ye fix up that oul' craither's head a bit?' Jamie asked.

I brought over the bogman's coat. Anna made a pillow of it and placed it under his head. He turned over on his side. As he did so a handful of small change rolled out of his pocket.

'Think of that now,' Jamie said, as he gathered it up and stuffed it back where it belonged, 'an oul' dhrunken turf dhriver wi' money t' waste while we're starvin'.'

From that moment we were acutely hungry.

This new incident rendered the condition poignant.

'Maybe Mrs Boyle an' th' wains are as hungry as we are,' Anna remarked.

'Wi' a bogful o' turf at th' doore?'

'Th' can't eat turf, Jamie!'

'Th' can warm their shins, that's more'n we can do, in a minute or two.'

The rapidly diminishing coals were arranged once more. They were a mere handful now, and the house was cold.

There were two big holes in the chimney where Jamie kept old pipes, pipe cleaners, bits of rags, and scraps of tobacco. He liked to hide a scrap or two there, and in times of scarcity make himself believe he *found* them. His last puff of smoke had gone up the chimney hours ago. He searched both holes without success. A bright idea struck him. He searched for Boyle's pipe. He searched in vain.

'Holy Moses!' he exclaimed, 'what a breath; a pint ov that wud make a mule dhrunk!'

'Thry it, Jamie,' Anna said, laughing.

'Thry it yerself—yer a good dale more ov a judge,' he said snappishly.

A wild gust of wind came down the chimney and blew the loose ashes off the hearth. Jamie ensconced himself in his corner—a picture of dispair.

'I wondther if Billy O'Hare's in bed?' he said.

'Ye'd need fumigatin' afther smokin' Billy's tobacco, Jamie!'

'I'd smoke tobacco scraped out o' the breeches-pocket ov th' oul' divil in hell!' he replied.

He arose, put on his muffler, and made ready to visit the sweep. On the way to the door another idea turned him back. He put on the bogman's overcoat and rabbit-skin cap. Anna, divining his intention, said: 'That's th' first sign of sense I've seen in you for a month of Sundays.'

'Ye cudn't see it in a month ov Easter Sundays, anyway,' he retorted, with a superior toss of his head.

Anna kept up a rapid fire of witty remarks. She injected humour into the situation and laughed like a girl, and although she felt the pangs more keenly than any of us, her laughter was genuine and natural.

Jamie had his empty pipe in his mouth, and by force of habit he picked up in the tongs a little bit of live coal to light it. We all tittered.

'Th' h—l!' he muttered, as he made for the door. Before he reached it my sister walked in. McGuckin wasn't at home. His wife couldn't pay. We saw the whole story on her face, every pang of it. Her eyes were red and swollen. Before she got out a sentence of the tale of woe, she noticed the old man in Boyle's clothing and burst out laughing. So hearty and boisterous was it that we all again caught the contagion and laughed with her. Sorrow was deep-seated. It had its roots away down at the bottom of things, but laughter was always up near the surface and could be tapped on the slightest provocation. It was a by-valve—a way of escape for the overflow. There were times when sorrow was too deep for tears. But there never was a time when we couldn't laugh!

People in our town who expected visitors to knock, provided a knocker. The knocker was a distinct line of social demarcation. We lived below the line. The minister and the tract distributor were the only persons who ever knocked at our door.

Scarcely had our laughter died away when the door opened and there entered in the sweep of a blizzard's tail Billy O'Hare. The gust of cold winter wind made us shiver again, and we drew up closer to the dying fire—so small now as to be seen with difficulty.

'Be th' seven crosses ov Arbow, Jamie,' he said, 'I'm glad yer awake, me bhoy; if ye hadn't I'd haave pulled ye out be th' tail ov yer shirt!'

'I was jist within an ace ov goin' over an' pullin' ye out be th' heels myself.'

The chimney-sweep stepped forward and, tapping Jamie on the forehead, said: 'Two great minds workin' on th' same thought shud produce wondtherful results, Jamie; lend me a chew ov tobacco!'

'Ye've had larks for supper, Billy; yer jokin'!' Jamie said.

'Larks be d—d,' Billy said, 'm' tongue's stickin' t' th' roof ov me mouth!'

Again we laughed, while the two men stood looking at each other—speechless.

'Ye can do switherin' as easy sittin' as standin',' Anna said, and Billy sat down.

The bogman's story was repeated in minutest detail. The sweep scratched his sooty head and looked wise.

'It's gone!' Anna said quietly, and we all looked toward the fire. It was dead. The last spark had been extinguished. We shivered.

'We don't need so many stools aanyway,' Jamie said. 'I'll get a hatchet an' we'll haave a fire in no time.'

'T' be freezin' t' death wi' a bogman goin' t' waste is unChristian, t' say th' laste,' Billy ventured.

'Every time we get to th' end of th' tether God appears!' Anna said reassuredly, as she pinned her shawl closer around her neck.

'There's nothin' but empty bowels and empty pipes in our house,' the sweep said, 'but we've got half a dozen good turf left!'

'Well, it's a long lane that's got no turnin'—ye might lend us thim,' Jamie suggested.

'If ye'll excuse m' fur a minit, I'll warm this house, an' may the Virgin choke m' in th' nixt chimley I sweep if I don't!'

In a few minutes he returned with six black turf. The fire was rebuilt, and we basked in its warm white glow. The bogman snored on. Billy inquired about the amount of his change. Then he became solicitous about his comfort on the floor. Each suggestion was a furtive flank movement on Boyle's loose change.

Anna saw the bent of his mind and tried to divert his attention.

'Did ye ever hear, Billy,' she said, 'that if we stand a dhrunk maan on his head it sobers him?'

'Be the powers, no.'

'They say,' she said, with a twinkle in her eyes, 'that it empties him of his contents.'

'Ay,' sighed the sweep; 'there's something in that, Anna; let's thry it on Boyle.'

There was an element of excitement in the suggestion and we youngsters hoped it would be carried out. Billy made a move to suit the action to the thought, but Anna pushed him gently back.

'Jamie's mouth is as wathry as yours, Billy, but we'll take no short cuts, we'll go th' long way around.'

That seemed a death-blow to hope. My sisters began to whimper and sniffle. We had many devices for diverting hunger. The one always used as a last resort was the stories of the 'great famine'. We were particularly helped by one about a family half of whom died around a pot of stir-about that had come too late. When we heard Jamie say, 'Things are purty bad, but they're not as bad as they might be,' we knew a famine story was on the way.

'Hould yer horses there a minute!' Billy O'Hare broke in. He took the step-ladder and before we knew what he was about he had taken a bunch of dried rosemary from the roof-beams and was rubbing it in his hands as a substitute for tobacco.

After rubbing it between his hands, he filled his pipe and began to puff vigorously.

'Wud ye luk at 'im!' Jamie exclaimed.

'I've lived with th' mother ov invintion since I was th' size ov a mushroom,' he said between the puffs, 'an' begorra she's betther nor a wife.'

The odour filled the house. It was like the sweet incense of a censer. The men laughed and joked over the discovery. The sweep indulged himself in some extravagant self-laudatory statements, one of which became a household word with us.

'Jamie,' he said, as he removed his pipe and looked seriously at my father, 'who was that poltroon that discovered tobacco?'

Anna informed him.

'What'll become ov 'im whin compared wid O'Hare, th' inventor of th' rosemary delection? I ax ye, Jamie, bekase ye're an honest maan.'

'Heaven knows, Billy.'

'Ay, Heaven only knows, fur I'll hand down t' m' future ancestors the O'Hare brand ov rosemary tobacco!'

'Wondtherful, wondtherful!' Jamie said, in mock solemnity.

'Ay, t' think,' Anna said, 'that ye invinted it in our house!'

We forgot our hunger pangs in the excitement. Jamie filled his pipe, and the two men smoked for a few minutes. Then a fly appeared in the precious ointment. My father took his pipe out of his mouth and looked inquisitively at Billy.

'M' head's spinnin' 'round like a peerie!' he exclaimed.

'Whin did ye ate anything?' asked the sweep.

'Yestherday.'

'Ay, well, it's th' mate ye haaven't in yer bowels that's makin' ye feel quare.'

'What's th' matther wi' th' invintor?' Anna asked.

Billy had removed his pipe and was staring vacantly into space.

'I'm seein' things two at a time, b' Jazus!' he answered.

'We've got plenty of nothin' but wather, maybe ye'd like a good drink, Billy?'

Before he could reply the bogman raised himself to a half-sitting posture, and yelled with all the power of his lungs: 'Whoa! back, ye dhirty baste, back!'

The wild yell chilled the blood in our veins.

He sat up, looked at the black figure of the sweep for a moment, then he made a spring at Billy, and before any one could interfere poor Billy had been felled to the floor with a terrible smash on the jaw. Then he jumped on him. We youngsters raised a howl that awoke the sleepers in Pogue's Entry. Jamie and Billy soon overpowered Boyle. When the neighbours arrived they found O'Hare sitting on Boyle's neck and Jamie on his legs.

'Where am I?' Boyle asked.

'In the home of friends,' Anna answered.

'Wud th' frien's donate a mouthful ov breath?'

He was let up. The story of the night was told to him. He listened attentively. When the story was told he thrust his hand into his pocket and brought forth some change.

'Hould yer han' out, ye black imp o' hell,' he said to O'Hare.

The sweep obeyed, but remarked that the town clock had already struck twelve.

'I don't care a d—n if it's thirteen!' he said. 'That's fur bread, that's fur tay, that's fur tobacco, an' that's fur somethin' that runs down yer throat like a rasp,

100

fur me. Now don't let th' grass grow undther yer flat feet, ye divil.'

After some minor instructions from Anna, the sweep went off on his midnight errand. The neighbours were sent home. The kettle replaced the pot on the chain, and we gathered full of ecstasy close to the fire.

'Whisht!' Anna said.

We listened. Above the roar of the wind and the rattling of the casement we heard a loud noise.

'It's Billy dundtherin' at Marget Hurll's doore,' Jamie said.

O'Hare arrived with a bang! He put his bundles down on the table and vigorously swung his arms like flails around him to thaw himself out. Anna arranged the table and prepared the meal. Billy and Jamie went at the tobacco. Boyle took the whiskey and said: 'I thank my God an' the holy angels that I'm in th' house ov timperance payple!' Then looking at Jamie, he said: 'Here's t' ye, Jamie, an' ye, Anna, an' th' scoundthrel O'Hare, an' here's t' th' three that niver bred, th' priest, th' pope, an' th' mule!'

Then at a draught he emptied the bottle and threw it behind the fire, grunting his satisfaction.

'Wudn't that make a corpse turn 'round in his coffin?' Billy said.

'Keep yer eye on that loaf, Billy, or he'll be dhrinkin' our health in it!' Jamie remarked humourously.

Boyle stretched himself out on the floor and yawned. The little table was brought near the fire, the loaf was cut in slices and divided. It was a scene that brought us to the edge of tears—tears of joy. Anna's face particularly beamed. She talked as she prepared, and her talk was of God's appearance at the end of every tether, and of the silver lining on the edge of every cloud. She had a penchant for mottoes, but she never used them in a siege. It was when the siege was broken she poured them in and they found a welcome. As she spoke of God bringing relief, Boyle got up on his haunches.

'Anna,' he said, 'if aanybody brot me here th' night it was th' oul' divil in hell.'

''Deed yer mistaken, Felix,' she answered sweetly. 'When God sends a maan aanywhere he always gets there, even if he has to be taken there by th' divil.'

When all was ready we gathered around the table.

'How I wish we could sing!' she said, as she looked at us.

The answer was on every face. Hunger would not wait on ceremony. We were awed into stillness and silence, however, when she raised her hand in benediction. We bowed our heads. Boyle crossed himself.

'Father,' she said, 'we thank Thee for sendin' our friend Felix here th' night. Bless his wife an' wains, bless them in basket an' store, an' take good care of his oul' mare. Amen!'

Chapter 8
THE WIND BLOWETH
WHERE IT LISTETH

I sat on a fence in a potato field, whittling an alder stick into a pea-blower one afternoon in the early autumn, when I noticed at the other end of the field the well-known figure of 'the master'. He was dressed as usual in light grey, and as usual rode a fine horse. I dropped off the fence as if I had been shot. He urged the horse to a gallop. I pushed the clumps of red hair under my cap and pressed it down tightly on my head. Then I adjusted the string that served as a suspender. On came the galloping horse. A few more lightning touches to what covered my nakedness and he reined up in front of me! I straightened up like a piece of whalebone!'

'What are ye doing?' he asked in that far-off imperious voice of his.

'Kapin' th' crows off th' pirtas, yer honour.'

'You need a new shirt!' he said.

The blood rushed to my face. I tried to answer, but the attempt seemed to choke me.

'You need a new shirt!' he almost yelled at me.

I saw a smile playing about the corners of his fine large eyes. It gave me courage.

'Ay, yer honour, 'deed that's thrue.'

'Why don't you get one?'

The answer left my mind and travelled like a flash to the glottis, but that part of the machinery was out of order, and the answer hung fire. I paused, drew a long breath and strained the string. Then matching his thin smile with a thick grin, I replied: 'Did yer honour iver work fur four shillin's a week and share it wid nine others?'

'No!' he said, and the imprisoned smile was released.

'Well, if ye iver do, shure ye'll be lucky to haave skin, let alone shirt!'

'You consider yourself lucky, then?'

'Ay, middlin'.'

He galloped away and I lay down flat on my back, wiped the sweat from my brow with the sleeve of my jacket, turned the hair loose, and eased up the string.

That night, at the first sound of the farmyard bell, I took to my heels through the fields, through the yard, and down the Belfast road to Withero's stone-pile. Willie was just quitting for the day. I was almost breathless, but I blurted out what then seemed to me the most important happening in my life.

Willie took his eye-protectors off and looked at me.

'So ye had a crack wi' the masther, did ye?'

'Ay, quite a crack.'

'He mistuk ye fur a horse!' he said.

This damper on my enthusiasm drew an instant reply.

''Deed no, nor an ass naither.'

Willie bundled up his hammers and prepared to go home. He took out his flint and steel. Over the flint he laid a piece of brown paper, chemically treated, then he struck the flint a sharp blow with his steel; a spark was produced, the spark ignited the paper, it began to burn in a smouldering blazeless way; he stuffed the paper into the bowl of his pipe, and began the smoke that was to carry him over the journey home. I shouldered some of his hammers and we trudged along the road toward Antrim.

'Throth, I know yer no ass, me bhoy, though Jamie's a good dale of a mule, but yer Ma's got wit enough fur the family. That answer ye gave Misther Chaine was from yer Ma. It was gey cute an'll git ye a job, I'll bate.'

I had something else to tell him, but I dreaded his critical mind. When we got to the railway bridge he laid his hammers on the wall while he relit his pipe. I saw my last opportunity and seized it.

'Say, Willie, did ye iver haave a feelin' that made ye feel fine all over, and—and—made ye pray?'

'I niver pray,' he said. 'These wathery-mouthed gossoons who pray air jist like oul' Hughie Thornton wi' his pockets bulgin' wi' scroof (crusts). They're naggin' at God from Aysther t' Christmas t' fill their pockets! A good day's stone-breakin' 's my prayer. At night I jist say, "Thank ye, Father!" In th' mornin' I say, 'Morra, Father, how's all up aroun' th' throne this mornin'?" '

'An' does He spake t' ye back?'

'Ov coorse, d'ye think He's got worse manners nor me? He says, "Hallo, Willie," says He. "How's it wi' ye this fine mornin'?" "Purty fine, Father, purty fine," says I. But tell me, bhoy, was there a girl aroun' whin that feelin' struck ye?'

'Divil a girl, at all!'

'Them feelin's sometimes comes from a girl, ye know. I had wan wanst, but that's a long story, heigh ho; ay, that's a long story!'

'Did she die, Willie?'

'Never mind her. That feelin' may haave been from God. Yer Ma hes a quare notion that wan chile of her'n will be inclined that way. She's dhrawn eleven blanks, maybe she's dhrawn a prize, afther all; who knows.'

Old McCabe, the road mender, overtook us, and for the rest of the journey I was seen but not heard.

That night I sat by her side in the chimney-corner and recited the events of the day. It had been full of magic, mystery, and meaning to me. The meaning was a little clearer to me after the recital.

'Withero sometimes talks like a ha'penny book wi' no laves in it,' she said. 'But most of the time he's nearer the facts than most of us. It isn't all blether, dear.'

We sat up late, long after the others had gone to sleep. She read softly a chapter of *Pilgrim's Progress,* the chapter in which he is relieved of his burden. I see now that woodcut of a gate and over the gate the words: 'Knock and it shall be opened unto you.' She had read it before. I was familiar with it, but in the light of that day's experience it had a new meaning. She warned me, however, that my name was neither Pilgrim nor Withero, and in elucidating her meaning she explained the phrase, 'The wind bloweth where it listeth.' I learned to listen for the sound thereof, and I wondered from whence it came, not only the wind of the heavens, but the spirit that moved men in so many directions.

The last act of that memorable night was the making of a picture. It took many years to find out its meaning, but every stroke of the brush is as plain to me now as they were then.

'Ye'll do somethin' for me?'

'Ay, aanything in th' world.'

'Ye won't glunch nor ask questions?'

'Not a question.'

'Shut yer eyes an' stan' close t' th' table.'

I obeyed. She put into each hand a smooth stick with which Jamie had smoothed the soles of our shoes.

'Jist for th' now there are the handles of a plough. Keep yer eyes shut tight. Ye've seen a maan ploughin' a field?'

'Ay.'

'Think that ye see a long, long field. Ye're ploughin' it. The other end is so far away ye can't see it. Ye see a wee bit of the furrow, jist a wee bit. Squeeze th' plough handles.'

I squeezed.

'D'ye see th' trees yonder?'

'Ay.'

'An' th' birds pickin' in th' furrow?'

'A-y.'

She took the sticks away and gently pushed me on a stool and told me I might open my eyes.

'That's quare,' I said.

'Listen, dear, ye've put yer han' t' th' plough; ye must niver, niver take it away. All through life ye'll haave thim plough handles in yer han's, an' ye'll be goin' down th' furrow. Ye'll crack a stone here and there, th' plough'll stick often an' things'll be out of gear, but yer in th' furrow all the time. Ye'll change horses, ye'll change clothes, ye'll change yerself, but ye'll always be in the furrow, ploughin', ploughin', ploughin'! I'll go a bit of th' way, Jamie'll go a bit, yer brothers an' sisters a bit, but we'll dhrap out wan b' wan. Ye're God's ploughmaan.'

As I stood to say good-night she put her hand on my head and muttered something that was not intended for me to hear. Then she kissed me good-night, and I climbed to my pallet under the thatch.

I was afraid to sleep, lest the 'feelin'' should take

wings. When I was convinced that some of it, at least, would remain, I tried to sleep and couldn't. The mingled ecstasy and excitement was too intense. I heard the town clock strike the hours far into the morning.

Before she awoke next morning I had exhausted every agency in the house that would co-ordinate flesh and spirit. When I was ready I tiptoed to her bedside and touched her on the cheek. Instantly she awoke and sat upright. I put my hands on my hips and danced before her. It was a noiseless dance with bare feet on the mud floor.

Her long thin arms shot out toward me, and I buried myself in them.

'So it stayed,' she whispered in my ear.

'Ay, an' there's more of it.'

She arose and dressed quickly. A live coal was scraped out of the ashes and a turf fire built around it. My feet were winged as I flew to the town well for water. When I returned she had several slices of toast ready. Toast was a luxury. Of course, there was always—or nearly always—bread, and often there was butter, but toast to the very poor in those days wasn't merely a matter of bread and butter, fire and time! It was more often inclination that turned the balance for or against it, and inclination always came on the back of some emotion, chance or circumstance. Here all the elements met and the result was toast.

I took a mouthful of her tea out of her cup; she reciprocated. We were like children. Maybe we were. Love tipped our tongues, winged our feet, opened our hearts and hands, and permeated every thought and act. She stood at the mouth of the entry until I disappeared at the town head. While I was yet within sight I looked back half a dozen times, and we waved our hands.

It was nearly a year before a dark line entered this spiritual spectrum. It was inevitable that such a mental condition—ever in search of a larger expression—should gravitate towards the Church. It has seemed also that it was just as inevitable that the best thought of which the Church has been the custodian should be crystallised into a creed. I was promoted to the 'big house'. There, of course, I was overhauled and put in touch with the fittings and furniture. As a flunkey I had my first dose of boiled linen, and I liked it.

I was enabled now to attend church and Sunday School. Indeed, I would have gone there, religion or no religion, for where else could I have sported a white shirt and collar? With my boiled linen and my brain stuffed with texts, I gradually drew away from the chimney-corner and never again did I help Willie Withero to carry his hammers. Ah, if one could only go over life and correct the mistakes.

Gradually I lost the warm human feeling and sub-stituted for it a theology. I began to look upon my mother as one about whose salvation there was some doubt. I urged her to attend church. Forms and ceremonies became the all-important things, and the life and the spirit were proportionately unimportant. I became mildewed with the blight of respectability. I became the possessor of a hard hat that I might ape the respectables. I walked home every night from Ballycraigie with Jamie Wallace, and Jamie was the best-dressed working-man in the town. I was treading a well-worn pathway. I was 'getting on'. A good slice of my new religion consisted in excellency of service to my employers—my 'betters'. Preacher,

109

priest, and peasant thought alike on these topics. Anna was pleased to see me in a new garb, but she noticed, and I noticed, that I had grown away from the corner. In the light of my new adjustment I saw *duties* plainer, but duty may become a hammer by which affection may be beaten to death.

I imagined the plough was going nicely in the furrow, for I wasn't conscious of striking any snags or stones, but Anna said: 'A ploughman who skims th' surface of th' sod strikes no stones, dear, but it's because he isn't ploughin' *deep*!'

I have ploughed deep enough since, but too late to go back and compare notes.

She was pained, but tried to hide it. If she was on the point of tears she would tell a funny story.

'Acushla,' she said to me one night, after a theological discussion, 'sure ye remind me of a ducklin' hatched by a hen.'

'Why?'

'We're at home in conthrary elements. Ye use texts t' fight with, an' I use them to get pace of heart!'

'Are you wiser nor Mr Holmes, an' William Brennan and Miss McGee?' I asked. 'Them's th' ones that think as I do—I mane I think as they do!'

'No, 'deed I'm not as wise as aany of thim, but standin' outside a wee bit I can see things can't be seen inside. Forby they haave no special pathway t' God that's shut t' me, nor yer oul' father, nor Willie Withero.'

Sometimes Jamie took a hand. Once, when he thought Anna was going to cry, in an argument, he wheeled around in his seat and delivered himself.

'I'll tell ye, Anna, that whelp needs a good argyment wi' th' tongs! Jist take thim an' hit 'im a skite on the jaw wi' thim an' I'll say, "Amen". '

'That's no clinch to an argyment,' I said, 'an' thruth is thruth!'

'Ay, an' tongs is tongs! An' some o' ye young upstarts whin ye git a dickey on an' a choke-me-tight collar think yer jist ready t' sit down t' tay wi' God!'

Anna explained, and gave me more credit than was due me. So Jamie ended the colloquy by the usual cap to his every climax.

'Well, what th' — do I know about thim things, aanyway? Let's haave a good cup o' tay, an' say no more about it!'

The more texts I knew, the more fanatical I became. And the more of a fanatic I was, the wider grew the chasm that divided me from my mother. I talked as if I knew 'every saint in heaven and every divil in hell.'

She was more than patient with me, though my spiritual conceit must have given her many a pang. Antrim was just beginning to get accustomed to my habiliments of boots, boiled linen, and hat, when I left to 'push my fortune' in other parts. My enthusiasm had its good qualities too, and she was quick to recognise them, quicker than to notice its blemishes. My last hours in the town—on the eve of my first departure—I spent with her.

'I feel about you, dear,' she said, laughing, 'as Micky Free did about the soul of his father in Purgatory. He had been payin' for masses for what seemed to him an uncommonly long time.

'How's th' oul' bhoy gettin' on?' Micky asked the priest.

' "Purty well, Micky, his head is out.'

' "Begorra, thin, I know th' rist ov 'im will be out soon—I'll pay for no more masses!"

'Your head is up and out from the bottom of th'

world, and I haave faith that ye'll purty soon be all
out, an' some day ye'll get the larger view, for ye'll be
in a larger place an' ye'll haave seen more of people
an' more of the world.'

I have two letters of that period. One I wrote her
from Jerusalem in the year 1884. As I read the
yellow childish epistle I am stung with remorse that
it is full of the narrow sectariansim that still held me
in its grip. The other is dated Antrim, July, 1884,
and is her answer to my sectarian appeal.

'Dear Boy,' she says, 'Antrim has had many
soldier sons in far-off lands, but you are the first, I
think, to have the privilege of visiting the Holy
Land. Jamie and I are proud of you. All the old
friends have read your letter. They can hardly
believe it. Don't worry about our souls. When we
come one by one in the twilight of life, each of us,
Jamie and I, will have our sheaves. They will be little
ones, but we are little people. I want no glory here or
hereafter that Jamie cannot share. I gave God a
ploughman, but your father says I must chalk half of
that to his account. Hold tight the handles and
plough deep. We watch the candle and every wee
spark thrills our hearts, for we know it's a letter from
you.
                    Your loving Mother.'

Chapter 9
'BEYOND TH' MEADOWS AN' TH' CLOUDS'

When the bill-boards announced that I was to deliver a lecture on 'England in the Sudan' in the only hall in the town, Antrim turned out to satisfy its curiosity. 'How doth this man know, not having learned?' the wise ones said, for when I shook the dust of its blessed streets from my brogues seven years previously, I was an illiterate.

Anna could have told them, but none of the wise knew her, for curiously enough to those who knew of her existence, but had never seen her, she was known as 'Jamie's wife'. Butchers and bakers and candlestick makers were there; several ministers, some quality, near quality, the inhabitants of the entries in the 'Scotch quarter', and all the newsboys in town. The fact that I personally bribed the newsboys accounted for their presence. I bought them out and reserved the front seats for them. It was in the way of a class reunion with me. Billy O'Hare had gone beyond—where there are no chimneys, and Ann where she could keep clean: they were both dead. Many of the old familiar faces were absent, they, too, had gone—some to other lands, some to another world. Jamie was there. He sat between Willie Withero and Ben Baxter. He heard little of what was said, and understood less of what he heard. The vicar, Mr Holmes, presided. There was a vote of thanks, followed by the customary seconding by public men, then 'God save the Queen', and I went home to tell Anna about it.

Jamie took one arm and Withero clung to the other.

'Jamie,' shouted Withero in a voice that could be heard by the crowd that followed us, 'd'ye mind th' first time I seen ye wi' Anna?'

'Ay, 'deed I do!'

'Ye didn't know it was in 'er, did ye, Jamie?'

'Yer a liar, Willie; I know'd frum th' minute I clapped eyes on 'er that she was th' finest wuman on God's futstool!'

'Ye can haave whativer benefit ov th' doubt there is, Jamie, but jist th' same any oul' throllop can be a father, but by G— it takes a rale wuman t' be th' mother ov a rale maan! Put that in yer pip an' smoke it.'

'He seems t' think,' said Jamie, appealing to me, 'that only quality can produce fine childther!'

'Yer spakin' ov clothes, Jamie; I'm spakin' ov mind, an' ye wor behind th' doore whin th' wor givin' it out, but begorra, Anna was at th' head ov th' class, an' that's no feerie story, naither is it, me bhoy!'

At the head of Pogue's Entry, Bob Dougherty, Tommy Wilson, Sam Manderson, Lucinda Gordon, and a dozen others stopped for a 'partin' crack'.

The kettle was boiling on the chain. The hearth had been swept and a new coat of whitening applied. There was a candle burning in her sconce and the thin yellow rays lit up the glory on her face—a glory that was encased in a newly-tallied white cap. My sister sat on one side of the fireplace, and she on the other—in her corner. I did not wonder, I did not ask why they did not make a supreme effort to attend the lecture—I knew. They were more supremely

115

interested than I was. They had never heard a member of the family or a relative speak in public, and their last chance had passed by. There they were, in the light of a peat fire and the tallow dip, supremely happy.

The neighbours came in for a word with Anna. They filled the space. The stools and creepies were all occupied.

'Sit down, Willie,' my father said. 'Take a nice cushioned chair an' be at home.'

Withero was leaning against the table. He saw and was equal to the joke.

'Whin nature put a pilla on maan, it was intinded fur t' sit on th' groun', Jamie!' And he sat on the mud floor.

'It's th' proud wuman ye shud be th' night,' Marget Hurll said, 'an' Misther Armstrong it was that said it was proud th' town shud be t' turn out a boy like him!'

Withero took his pipe out of his mouth and spat in the ashes—as a preface to a few remarks.

'Ay,' he grunted, 'I cocked m' ears up an' dunched oul' Jamie whin Armshtrong said that. Jamie couldn't hear it, so I whispered t' my'self, "Begorra, if a wee fella turns *up* whin Anthrim turns 'im out, it's little credit t' Anthrim, I'm thinkin'!" '

Anna laughed, and Jamie, putting his hand behind his ear, asked: 'What's that—what's that?'

The name and remarks of the gentlemen who seconded the vote of thanks were repeated to him.

'Ha, ha, ha!' he laughed, as he slapped me on the knee. 'Well, well, well, if that wudn't make a brass monkey laugh!'

'Say,' he said to me, 'd'ye mind th' night ye come home covered wi' clabber——'

'Whisht!' I said, as I put my mouth to his ear. 'I only want to mind that he had three very beautiful daughters.'

'Did ye iver spake t' aany o' thim?' Jamie asked.

'Yes.'

'Whin?'

'When I sold them papers.'

'Ha, ha, a ha'penny connection, eh?'

'It's betther t' mind three fine things about a maan than wan mean thing, Jamie,' Anna said.

'If both o' ye's on me, I'm bate,' he said.

'Stop yer palaver an' let's haave a story ov th' war wi' th' naygars in Egypt,' Mrs Hurll said.

'Ay, that's right,' one of the Gainer boys said. 'Tell us what the queen give ye a medal fur!'

They wanted a story of blood, so I smeared the tale red. When I finished Anna said, 'Now tell thim, dear, what ye tuk th' shillin' fur!'

'You tell them, mother.'

'You tuk it t' fight ignorance an' not naygars, didn't ye?'

'Yes, but the fight continues.'

'Ay, with you, but——'

'Ah, never mind, mother, I have taken it up where you laid it down, and long after——'

That was as far as I got, for Jamie exploded just then and said: 'Now, get t' h——l home, ivery wan o' ye, an' give's a minute wi' 'im jist for ourselves, will ye?'

He said it with laughter in his voice and it sounded in the ears of those present as polite and pleasing as anything in the domain of their amenities.

They arose as one, all except Withero, and he couldn't, for Jamie gripped him by a leg and held him on the floor just as he sat.

In their good-night expressions, the neighbours unconsciously revealed what the lecture and the story meant to them. Summed up, it meant, 'Sure it's jist wondtherful ye warn't shot!'

'When we were alone, alone with Withero, Mary 'wet' a pot of tea, and warmed up a few farrels of fadge, and we commenced. Little was said, but feeling ran high. It was like a midnight mass. Anna was silent, but there were tears, and as I held her in my arms and kissed them away, Jamie was saying to Withero: 'Ye might take 'im fur a dandther out where ye broke whin we first met ye, Willie.'

'Ay,' Willie said, 'I'm m' own gaffer, I will that.'

I slept at Jamie Wallace's that night, and next morning took the 'dandther' with Withero up the Dublin road, past 'The Mount of Temptation' to the old stone-pile that was no longer a pile, but a hole in the side of the road. It was a sentimental journey that gave Willie a chance to say some things I knew he wanted to say.

'D'ye mind the pirta throusers Anna made ye once?'

'Yes, what of them?'

'Did ye iver think ye cud git used t' aanything if ye wor forced t' haave nothin' else for a while?'

'What's the point, Willie?'

'Sit down here awhile an' I'll tell ye.'

We sat down on the bank of the roadside. He took out his pipe, steel, and flint, filled his pipe, and talked as he filled.

'Me an' Jamie wor pirta sack people, purty d——d rough, too, but yer Ma was a piece ov fine linen frum the day she walked down this road wi' yer Dah till this minit whin she's waitin' fur ye in the corner. Ivery Sunday I've gone in jist t' hai a crack

wi' 'er an' d'ye know, bhoy, I got out o' that crack
somethin' good fur th' week. She was i'hell on saying
words precisely, but me an' Jamie wor too thick, an'
begorra she got used t' pirta sack words herself, but
she was i' fine linen jist the same.

'Wan day she says t' me, "Willie, says she, "ye see
people through dirty specs."

' "How's that?" says I.

' "I don't know," says she, "fur I don't wear yer
specs, but I think it's jist a poor habit ov yer mind.
Aych poor craither is made up ov some good an'
much that isn't s' good, an' ye see only what isn't s'
good!"

'Thin she towld m' somethin' which she niver
towld aanyone else, 'cept yer Dah, ov coorse.

' "Willie," says she, "fur twenty years I've seen the
Son of Maan ivery day ov m' life!"

' "How's that?" says I.

' "I've more'n seen 'im. I've made tay fur 'im, an'
broth on Sunday. I've mended 'is oul' duds, washed
'is dhirty clothes, shuk 'is han', stroked 'is hair, an'
said kind words to 'im!"

' "God Almighty!" says I, "yer goin' mad, Anna!"

'She tuk her oul' Bible an' read t' me these words; I
mind them well: "Whin ye do it t' wan o' these
craithers ye do it t' me!"

'Well, me bhoy, I thunk an' thunk over thim words,
and wud ye believe it, I begun t' clane m' specs. Wan
day th' "Dummy" came along t' m' stone-pile. Ye
mind 'er, don't ye?' (The Dummy was a harlot, who
lived in the woods up the Dublin road in summer, and
Heaven only knows where in winter).

'Th' Dummy,' Willie continued, 'came over t' th'
pile an' acted purty gay, but says I, "Dummy, if
there's anythin' I kin give ye I'll give it, but ther's
nothin' ye kin give me!"

119

' "Ye break stones fur a livin'," says she.

' "Ay," says I.

' "What wud ye do if ye wor a lone wuman an' cudn't get nothin' at all t' do?"

' "I dunno," says I.

' "I don't want to argufy or palaver wi' a dacent maan," says she, "but I'm terrible hungry."

' "Luk here," says I, "I've got a dozen pirtas I'm goin' t' roast fur m' dinner. I'll roast thim down there by that gate, an' I'll lave ye six an' a dhrink ov butthermilk. Whin ye see m' lave th' gate ye'll know yer dinner's ready."

' "God save ye," says she, "may yer meal barrel niver run empty, an' may yer bread foriver be rough-casted wi' butther!"

'I begun t' swither whin she left. Says I, "Withero, is yer specs clane? Kin ye see th' Son ov Maan in th' Dummy?" "Begorra, I dunno," says I t' me'self. I scratched m' head an' swithered till I thought m' brains wud turn t' stone.

'Says I t' m'self at last, "Ay, 'deed there must be th' spark there what Anna talks about!" Jist then I heard yer mother's voice as plain as I hear m' own now at this minute—an'what d'ye think Anna says?'

'I don't know, Willie.'

' "So ye haave th' Son ov Maan t' dinner th' day?"

' "Ay," says I.

' "An' givin' 'im yer lavins!"

'It was like a piece ov stone cuttin' the ball ov m' eye. It cut deep!

'I ran down th' road an' says I t' th' Dummy, "I'll tie a rag on a stick an' whin ye see m' wavin' it come an' take yer dinner, an' I'll take what's left!"

'I didn't wait fur no answer, but went and did what I shud.

'That summer when she was hungry she hung an oul' rag on th' thorn hedge down be the wee plantain where she camped, and I answered be a rag on a stick that she cud share mine and take hers first. One day I towld 'er yer mother's story about th' Son ov Maan. It was th' only time I ever talked wi' 'er. That winther she died in th' poorhouse, and before she died she sint me this.' He pulled out of an inside pocket a piece of paper, yellow with age, and so scuffed with handling that the scrawl was scarcely legible:

> *Mr Withero,*
> Stone breaker,
> Dublin Road,
> Antrim.

I seen Him in the ward last night, and I'm content to go now. God save you kindly.

> The Dummy.

Withero, having unburdened, we dandered down the road, through Masserene and home.

I proposed to Anna a little trip to Lough Neagh in a jaunting car.

'No, dear, it's no use; I want to mind it jist as Jamie and I saw it years an' years ago. I see it here in th' corner jist as plain as I saw it then; forby Antrim wud never get over th' shock of seein' me in a jauntin' car.'

'Then I'll tell you of a shorter journey. You have never seen the Steeple. It's the most perfect of all the Round Towers in Ireland, and just one mile from this corner. Now don't deny me the joy of taking you there. I'll guide you over the strand and away back of the poorhouse, out at the station, and then it's just a hundred yards or so!'

It took the combined efforts of Jamie, Withero, Mary, and me to persuade her, but she was finally persuaded, and dressed in a borrowed black knitted cap and her wee Sunday shawl, she set out with us.

'This is like a weddin',' Jamie said, as he tied the ribbons under her chin.

'Oh, it's worse, dear. It's a circus an' wake in wan, fur I'm about dead an' he's turned clown for a while.'

In five minutes everybody in Pogue's Entry heard the news. They stood at the door waiting to have a look.

Matty McGrath came in to see if there was 'aanythin' ' she could do.

'Ay,' Anna said, smiling, 'ye can go over an' tell oul' Ann Agnew where I'm goin', so she won't worry herself t' death findin' out!'

'She won't see ye,' Jamie said.

'She'd see a fly if it lit within a hundred yards of her!'

We went down the Kill Entry and over the rivulet we called 'the strand'. There were stepping stones in the water, and the passage was easy. As we crossed, she said: 'Right here was th' first place ye ever came t' see th' sun dance on th' water on Easter Sunday mornin'.'

We turned to the right and walked by the old burying-ground of the Unitarian meeting-house and past Mr Smith's garden. Next to Smith's garden was the garden of a cooper—I think his name was Farren.

'Right here,' I said, 'is where I committed my first crime!'

'What was it?' she asked.

'Stealing apples!'

'Ay, what a townful of criminals we had then!'

We reached the back of the poorhouse. Johnny Gardner was the master of it and 'goin' t' Johnny Gardner's' was understood as the last march of many of the inhabitants of Antrim, beginning with 'Tother Jack Welch', who was a sort of pauper *primus inter pares* of the town.

As we passed the little graveyard, we stood and looked over the fence at the little boards, all of one size and one pattern, that marked each grave.

'God in Heaven!' she exclaimed, 'isn't it fearful not to get rid of poverty even in death!'

I saw a shudder pass over her face, and I turned mine away.

Ten minutes later we emerged from the fields at the railway station.

'You've never seen Mr McKillop, the station-master, have you?' I asked.

'No.'

'Let us wait here for a minute, we may see him.'

'Oh, no, let's hurry on t' th' Steeple!'

So on we hurried.

It took a good deal of courage to enter when we got there, for the far-famed Round Tower of Antrim is *private property*. Around it is a stone wall enclosing the grounds of an estate. The tower stands near the house of the owner, and it takes temerity in the poor to enter. They seldom do enter, as a matter of fact, for they are not particularly interested in archaeology.

We timidly entered and walked up to the Tower.

'So that's th' Steeple!'

'Isn't it fine?'

'Ay, it's wondtherful, but wudn't it be nice t' take our boots off an' jist walk aroun' on this soft nice grass on our bare feet?'

The lawn was closely clipped and as level as a billiard table. The trees were dressed in their best summer clothing. Away in the distance we caught glimpses of an abundance of flowers. The air was full of the perfume of honeysuckle and sweet clover. Anna drank in the scenery with almost childish delight.

'D'ye think heaven will be as nice?' she asked.

'Maybe.'

'If it is, we will take our boots off an' sit down, won't we?' And she laughed like a girl.

'If there are boots in the next world,' I said, 'there will be cobblers, and you wouldn't want our old man to be a cobbler to all eternity?'

'You're right,' she said, 'nor afther spending seventy-five years here without bein' able to take my boots off an' walk on a nice lawn like this wud I care to spend eternity without that joy!'

'Do we miss what we've never had?'

'Ay, 'deed we do. I miss most what I've never had!'

'What, for instance?'

'Oh, I'll tell ye th' night when we're alone!'

We walked around the tower and ventured once beneath the branches of a big tree.

'If we lived here, d'ye know what I'd like t' do?'

'No.'

'Jist take our boots off an' play hide and go seek— wudn't it be fun?'

I laughed loudly.

'Whisht!' she said. 'They'll catch us if you make a noise!'

'You seem bent on getting your boots off,' I said laughingly.

Her reply struck me dumb.

'Honey,' she said, so softly and looking into my

124

eyes, 'do you realise that I have never stood on a patch of lawn in my life before?'

Hand in hand we walked toward the gate, taking an occasional, wistful glance back at the glory of the few, and thinking, both of us, of the millions of tired feet that never felt the softness of a smooth green sward.

At eight o'clock that night the door was shut *and barred.*

Jamie tacked several copies of the *Weekly Budget* over the window, and we were alone.

We talked of old times. We brought back the dead, and smiled or sighed over them. Old tales, of the winter nights of long ago, were retold with a new interest.

The town clock struck nine.

We sat in silence as we used to sit, while another sexton tolled off the days of the month after ringing the curfew.

'Many th' time ye've helter-skeltered home at th' sound of that bell!' she said.

'Yes, because the sound of the bell was always accompanied by a vision of a wet welt hanging over the edge of the tub!'

Jamie laughed and became reminiscent.

'D'ye mind what ye said wan time whin I bate ye wi' th' stirrup?'

'No, but I used to think a good deal more than I said.'

'Ay, but wan time I laid ye across m' knee an' gave ye a good shtrappin', then stud ye up an' says I, 'It hurts me worse than it hurts ye, ye divil!'

' "Ay," says you, "but it dizn't hurt ye in th' same place." '

'I don't remember, but from time immemorial boys have thought and said the same thing.'

'D'ye mind when *I* bate ye?' Anna asked, with a smile.

'Yes, I remember you solemnly promised Jamie you would punish me, and when he went down to Barney's you took a long straw and lashed me fearfully with it!'

The town clock struck ten.

Mary, who had sat silent all evening, kissed us all good-night and went to bed.

I was at the point of departure for the New World. Jamie wanted to know what I was going to do. I outlined an ambition, but its outworking was a problem. It was beyond his ken. He could not take in the scope of it. Anna could, for she had it from the day she first felt the movement of life in me. It was unpretentious—nothing the world would call great.

'Och, maan, but that wud be th' proud day fur Anna if ye cud do it.'

When the town clock struck eleven, Anna trembled.

'Yer cowld, Anna,' he said. 'I'll put on a few more turf.'

'There's plenty on dear; I'm not cold in my body.'

'Acushla, m' oul' hide's like a buffalo's or I'd see that ye want 'im t' yerself. I'm off t' bed!'

We sat in silence gazing into the peat fire. Memory led me back down the road to yesterday. She was out in the future and wandering in an unknown continent with only hope to guide her. Yet we must get together, and that quickly.

'Minutes are like fine gold now,' she said, 'an' my tongue seems glued, but I jist must spake.'

'We have plenty of time, mother.'

'Plenty!' she exclaimed. 'Every clang of th' town clock is a knife cuttin' th' cords—wan afther another—that bind me t' ye.'

127

'I want to know about your hope, your outlook, your religion,' I said.

'Th' biggest hope I've ever had was t' bear a chile that would love everybody as yer father loved me!'

'A sort of John-three-sixteen in miniature.'

'Ay.'

'The aim is high enough to begin with!'

'Not too high!'

'And your religion?'

'All in all, it's bein' kind an' lovin' kindness. *That* takes in God an' maan an' Pogue's Entry, an' th' world.'

The town clock struck twelve. Each clang 'a knife cutting a cord' and each heavier and sharper than the last. Each one vibrating, tingling, jarring along every nerve, sinew, and muscle. A feeling of numbness crept over me.

'That's the end of life for me,' she said slowly. There was a pause, longer and more intense than all the others. 'Maybe ye'll get rich an' forget.'

'Yes, I shall be rich. I shall be a millionaire—a millionaire of love, but no one shall ever take your place, dear!'

My overcoat served as a pillow. An old quilt made a pallet on the hard floor. I found myself being pressed gently down from the low creepie to the floor. I pretended to sleep. Her hot tears fell on my face. Her dear, toil-worn fingers were run gently through my hair. She was on her knees by my side. The tender mysticism of her youth came back and expressed itself in prayer. It was interspersed with tears and 'Ave Maria!'

When the first streak of dawn penetrated the old window we had our last cup of tea together, and later, when I held her in a long, lingering embrace, there were no tears—we had shed them all in the silence of the last vigil. When I was ready to go, she stood with her arm on the old yellow mantel-shelf. She was rigid and pale as death, but around her eyes and her mouth there played a smile. There was a look ineffable of maternal love.

'We shall meet again, mother,' I said.

'Ay, dearie, I know rightly we'll meet, but ochanee, it'll be out there beyond th' meadows an' th' clouds.'

Chapter 10

THE EMPTY CORNER

When I walked into Pogue's Entry about fifteen years later, it seemed like walking into another world—I was a foreigner.

'How quare ye spake!' Jamie said.

And Mary added demurely: 'Is it quality ye are that ye spake like it?'

'No, faith, not all,' I said, 'but it's the quality of America that makes me!'

'Think of that, now!' she exclaimed.

The neighbours came, new neighbours—a new generation, to most of whom I was a tradition. Other boys and girls had left Antrim for America, scores of them in the course of the years. There was a popular supposition that we all knew each other.

'Ye see th' Wilson bhoys ivery day, I'll bate,' Mrs Hainey said.

'No, I have never seen any of them.'

'Saints alive, how's that?'

'Because we live three thousand miles apart.'

'Ay, well, shure that 'ud be quite a dandther!'

'It didn't take ye long t' git a fortune, did it?' another asked.

'I never acquired a fortune such as you are thinking of.'

'Anna said you wor rich?'

'Anna was right, I am rich, but I was the richest boy in Antrim when I lived here.'

They looked dumbfounded.

'How's that?' Mrs Connor queried.

'Because Anna was my mother.'

I didn't want to discuss Anna at that time or to that gathering, so I gave the conversation a sudden turn and diplomatically led them in another direction. I explained how much easier it was for a policeman than a minister to make a 'fortune', and most Irishmen in America had a special bias toward law! Jamie had grown so deaf that he could only hear when I shouted into his ear. Visitors kept on coming, until the little house was uncomforably full.

'Wouldn't it be fine,' I shouted into Jamie's ear, 'if Billy O'Hare or Withero could just drop in now?'

'God save us all,' he said, 'th' oul' days an' oul' faces are gone foriver.'

After some hours of entertainment the uninvited guests were invited to go home.

I pulled Jamie's old tub out into the centre of the floor, and, taking my coat off, said gently: 'Now, good neighbours, I have travelled a long distance and need a bath, and if you don't mind I'll have one at once!'

The took it quite seriously and went home quickly. As soon as the house was cleared I shut and barred the door and Mary and I proceeded to prepare the evening meal.

I brought over the table and put it in its place near the fire. In looking over the old dresser I noticed several additions to the inventory I knew. The same old plates were there, many of them broken and arranged to appear whole. All holes, gashes, dents, and cracks were turned back or down to deceive the beholder. There were few whole pieces on the dresser.

'Great guns, Mary,' I exclaimed, 'here are two new plates and a new cup! Well, well, and you never said a word in any of your letters about them.'

'Ye needn't get huffed if we don't tell ye all the startlin' things!' Mary said.

'Ah!' I exclaimed, 'there's *her* cup!'

I took the precious thing from the shelf. The handle was gone, there was a gash at the lip and a few new cracks circling around the one I was familiar with twenty years previously.

What visions of the past came to me in front of that old dresser! How often in the long ago she had pushed that old cup gently toward me along the edge of the table—gently, to escape notice and avoid jealousy. Always at the bottom of it a teaspoonful of *her* tea and beneath the tea a bird's-eye-full of sugar. Each fairy picture of straggling tea leaves was our moving picture show of those old days. We all had tea leaves, but she had imagination. How we laughed and sighed and swithered over the fortunes spread out all over the inner surface of that cup!

'If ye stand there affrontin' our poor oul' delf all night we won't haave any tea at all!' Mary said.

The humour had gone from my face and speech from my tongue. I felt as one feels when he looks for the last time upon the face of his best friend. Mary laughed when I laid the old cup on a comparatively new saucer at my place. There was another laugh when I laid it out for customs inspection in the port of New York. I had a set of rather delicate after-dinner coffee cups. One bore the arms of Coventry in colours; another had the seal of St John's College, Oxford; one was from Edinburgh and another from Paris. They looked aristocratic. I laid them out in a row, and at the end of the row sat the proletarian, forlorn and battered—Anna's old tea-cup.

'What did you pay for this?' asked the inspector as he touched it contemptuously with his official toe.

'Never mind what I paid for it,' I replied, 'it's valued at a million dollars!'

The officer laughed, and I think the other cups laughed also, but they were not contemptuous; they were simply jealous.

Leisurely I went over the dresser, noting the new chips and cracks, handling them, maybe fondling some of them, and putting them as I found them.

'I'll jist take a cup o' tay,' Jamie said, 'I'm not feelin' fine.'

I had less appetite than he had, and Mary had less than either of us. So we sipped our tea for a while in silence.

'She didn't stay long afther ye left,' Jamie said, without looking up. Turning to Mary he continued, 'How long was it, aanyway, Mary?'

'Jist a wee while.'

'Ay, I know it wasn't long.'

'Did she suffer much?' I asked.

'She didn't suffer aany at all,' he said, 'she jist withered like th' laves on th' threes.'

'She jist hankered t' go,' Mary added.

'Wan night whin Mary was asleep,' Jamie continued, 'she read over agin yer letther—th' wan where ye wor spakin' so much about fishin'.'

'Ay,' I said, 'I had just been appointed missionary to a place called the Bowery, in New York, and I wrote her that I was no longer her ploughman, but her *fisher of men*.'

'Och, maan, if ye cud haave heard her laugh over th' different kinds of fishes ye wor catchin'! Iv'ry day for weeks she read it an' laughed an' cried over it.

'That night she says t' me, "Jamie," says she, "I don't care s' much fur fishers ov men as I do for th' ploughman."

' "Why?" says I.

' "Because," says she, "a gey good voice an' nice clothes will catch men, an' wimmin too, but it takes brains t' plough up th' superstitions ov th' ignorant."

' "There's somethin' in that," says I.

' "Tell 'im whin he comes," says she, "that I put th' handles ov a plough in his han's, an' he's t' let go ov thim only in death."

' "I'll tell 'm," says I, "but it's yerself that'll be here whin he comes," says I.

'She smiled like, an' says she, "What ye don't know, Jamie, wud make a pretty big library."

' "Ay," says I, 'I haaven't aany doubt ov that, Anna." '

There was a loud knock at the door.

'Let thim dundther,' Mary said.

He put his hand behind his ear and asked eagerly: 'What is 't?'

'Somebody's dundtherin'.'

'Let thim go t' h——,' he said angrily. 'Th' tuk 'im from Anna last time, th' won't take 'im from me an' you, Mary.'

Another and louder knock.

'It's Misthress Healy,' came a voice.

'Again his hand was behind his ear. The name was repeated to him.

'Misthress Healy, is it; well, I don' care a d——n if it was Misthress Toe-y!'

For a quarter of a century my sister has occupied my mother's chimney-corner, but it was vacant that night. She sat on my father's side of the fire. He and I sat opposite each other at the table—I on the same

134

spot, on the same stool where I used to sit when her cup towards the close of the meal came travelling along the edge of the table, and where her hand with a crust in it would sometimes blindly grope for mine.

But she was not there. In all my life I have never seen a space so empty!

My father was a peasant, with all the mental and physical characteristics of his class. My sister is a peasant woman who has been cursed with the same grinding poverty that cursed my mother's life. About my mother there was a subtlety of intellect and a spiritual quality that even in my ignorance was fascinating to me. I returned equipped to appreciate it, and she was gone. Gone, and a wide gulf lay between those left behind, a gulf bridged by the relation we have to the absent one more than by the relation we bore to each other.

We felt as keenly as others the kinship of the flesh, but there are kinships transcendentally higher, nobler, and of a purer nature than the nexus of the flesh. There were things to say that had to be left unsaid. They had not travelled that way. The language of my experience would have been a foreign tongue to them. *She* would have understood.

'Wan night by th' fire here,' Jamie said, taking the pipe out of his mouth, 'she says t' me, "Jamie," says she, "I'm clane done, jist clane done, an' I won't be long here."

' "Och, don't spake s' downmouthed, Anna," says I. "Shure ye'll feel fine in th' mornin'."

' "Don't palaver," says she, and she lukt terrible serious.

' "My God, Anna," says I, "ye wudn't be lavin' me alone," says I, "I can't thole it."

135

' "Yer more strong," says she, "an' ye'll live till he comes back—thin we'll be t'gether." '

He stopped there. He could go no further for several minutes.

'I hate a maan that gowls, but——'

'Go on,' I said, 'have a good one, and Mary and I will wash the cups and saucers.'

'D'ye know what he wants t' help me fur?' Mary asked, with her mouth close to his ear.'

'No.'

'He wants t' dhry thim so he can kiss *her* cup whin he wipes it! Kiss her *cup*, he mind; and right content with that!'

'I don't blame 'im,' said he, 'I'd kiss th' very groun' she walked on!'

As we proceeded to wash the cups, Mary asked: 'Diz th' ministhers in America wash dishes?'

'Some of them.'

'What kind?'

'My kind.'

'What do th' others do?'

'The big ones lay corner-stones and the little ones lay foundations.'

'Saints alive,' she said, 'an' what do th' hens do?'

'They clock' (hatch).

'Pavin' stones?'

'I didn't say pavin' stones!'

'Oh, ay,' she laughed loudly.

'Luk here,' Jamie said, 'I want t' laugh too. Now, what th' —— is't yer gigglin' at?'

I explained.

He smiled and said: 'Jazus, bhoy, that reminds me ov Anna, she cud say more funny things than aany wan I iver know'd.'

'And that reminds me,' I said, 'that the word you

have just misused *she* always pronounced with a caress.'

'Ay, I know rightly, but ye know I mane no harm, don't ye?'

'I know, but you remember when *she* used that word every letter in it was dressed in its best Sunday clothes, wasn't it?'

'Och, ay, an' I'd thravel twinty miles jist t' hear aany wan say it like Anna!'

'Well, I have travelled tens of thousands of miles, and I have heard the greatest preachers of the age, but I never heard any one pronouce it so beautifully!'

'But as I was a-sayin', bhoy, I haaven't had a rale good laugh since she died; haave I, Mary?'

'I haaven't naither,' Mary said.

'Ay, but ye've had double throuble, dear.'

'We never let trouble rob us of laughter when I was here.'

'Because whin ye wor here she was here too. In thim days whin throuble came she'd tear it t' pieces an' make fun ov aych piece, begorra. Ye might glour an' glunch, but ye'd haave t' laugh before th' finish—shure ye wud!'

The neighbours began to knock again. Some of the knocks were vocal and as plain as language. Some of the more familiar gaped in the window.

'Hes he hed 'is bath yit?' asked McGrath, the ragman.

We opened the door and in marched the inhabitants of our vicinity for the second 'crack'.

This right of mine own people to come and go as they pleased suggested to me the thought that if I wanted to have a private conversation with my father I would have to take him to another town.

The following day we went to the churchyard together—Jamie and I. Over her grave he had dragged a rough boulder, and on it in a straggling, unsteady, amateur hand were painted her initials, and below them his own. He was unable to speak there, and maybe it was just as well. I knew everything he wanted to say. It was written on his deeply furrowed face. I took his arm and led him away.

Our next call was at Willie Withero's stone-pile. There, when I remembered the nights that I passed in my new world of starched linen, too good to shoulder a bundle of his old hammers, I was filled with remorse. I uncovered my head and in an undertone muttered, 'God forgive me.'

'Great oul' bhoy was Willie,' he said.

'Ay.'

'Och, thim wor purty nice times whin he'd come in o' nights an' him an' Anna wud argie; but they're gone, clane gone, an' I'll soon be wi' thim.'

I bade farewell to Mary and took him to Belfast—for a private talk. Every day for a week we went out to the Cave Hill—to a wild and lonely spot where I had a radius of a mile for the sound of my voice. The thing of all things that I wanted him to know was that in America I had been engaged in the same fight with poverty that they were familiar with at home. It was hard for him to think of a wolf of hunger at the door of any home beyond the sea. It was astounding to him to learn that around me always there were thousands of ragged, starving people.

He just gaped and exclaimed: 'It's quare, isn't it?'

We sat on the grass on the hill-side, conscious each of us that we were saying the things one wants to say on the edge of the grave.

'She speyed I'd live t' see ye,' he said.

'She speyed well,' I answered.

'Th' night she died somethin' wondtherful happened t' me. I wasn't as deef as I am now, but I was purty deef. D'ye know, that night I cud hear th' aisiest whisper from her lips—I cud that. She groped fur m' han'; "Jamie," says she, "it's nearly over, dear."

' "God love ye," says I.

' "Ay," says she, "if He'll jist love me as ye've done, it'll be fine."

'Knowin' what a rough maan I'd been, I cudn't thole it.

' "The road's been gey rocky an' we've made many mistakes."

' "Ay, I said, "we've barged (scolded) a lot, Anna, but we didn't mane it."

' "No," says she, "our crock ov love was niver dhrained."

'I brot a candle in an' stuck it in th' sconce so's I cud see 'er face.

' "We might haave done betther," says she, "but sich a wee house, so many childther, an' so little money."

' "We war i' hard up,"

' "We were never hard up in love, wor we?"

' "No, Anna," says I, "but love dizn't boil th' kettle."

' "Wud ye rather haave a boilin' kittle than love if ye had t' choose?"

' "Och, no, not at all, ye know rightly I wudn't."

' "Forby, Jamie, we've given Antrim moren't such men than Lord Massarene."

' "What's that?" says I.

' "A maan that loves th' poorest craithers on earth an' serves thim."

'She had a gey good sleep afther that.

' "Jamie," says she, whin she awoke, "was I ravin'?"

' "Deed no, Anna," says I.

' "I'm not ravin' now, am I?"

' "Acushla, why do ye ask sich a question?"

' "Tell 'im I didn't like 'fisher of men' as well as 'th' ploughman'. It's aisy t' catch thim fish, it's hard t' plough up ignorance an' superstition—tell 'im that fur me, Jamie."

' "Ay, I'll tell 'im, dear."

' "Ye mind what I say'd t' ye on th' road t' Antrim, Jamie—that 'love is enough'?"

' "Ay."

' "I tell ye again wi' my dyin' breath."

'I leaned over an' kiss't 'er an'; she smiled at me. Ah, bhoy, if ye could haave seen that luk on 'er face, it was like a picture ov th' Virgin, it was that.

' "Tell the childther there's only wan kind of poverty, Jamie, an' that's t' haave no love in th' heart," says she.

' "Ay, I'll tell thim, Anna," says I.'

He choked up. The next thought that suggested itself for expression failed of utterance. The deep furrows on his face grew deeper. His lips trembled. When he could speak, he said: 'My God, bhoy, we had to beg a coffin t' bury 'er in!'

'If I had died at the same time,' I said, 'they would have had to do the same for me!'

'How quare,' he said.

I persuaded him to accompany me to one of the largest churches in Belfast. I was to preach there. That was more than he expected, and the joy of it was overpowering.

I do not remember the text, nor could I give at this

distance of time an outline of the discourse: it was one of those occasions when a man stands on the borderland of another world. I felt distinctly the spiritual guidance of an unseen hand. I took her theme and spoke more for her approval than for the approval of the crowd.

He could not hear, but he listened with his eyes. On the street, after the service, he became oblivious of time and place and people. He threw his long, lean arms around my neck and kissed me before a crowd. He hoped Anna was around listening. I told him she was, and he said he would like to be 'happed up' beside her, as he had nothing further to hope for in life.

In fear and trembling he crossed the Channel with me. In fear lest he should die in Scotland and they would not bury him in Antrim churchyard beside Anna. We visited my brothers and sisters for several days. Every day we took long walks along the country roads. These walks were full of questionings. Big vital questions of life and death and immortality.

They were quaintly put: 'There's a lot of balderdash about another world, bhoy. On yer oath, now, d'ye think there is wan?'

'I do.'

'If there is, wud He keep me frum Anna jist because I've been kinda rough?'

'I am sure He wouldn't!'

'He wudn't be s' d——d niggardly, wud He?'

'Never! God is love, and love doesn't work that way!'

At the railway station he was still pouring in his questions.

'D'ye believe in prayer?'

141

'Ay.'

'Well, jist ax sometimes that Anna an' me be together, will ye?'

'Ay.'

A little group of curious bystanders stood on the platform watching the little trembling old man clinging to me as the tendril of a vine clings to the trunk of a tree.

'We have just one minute, father.'

'Ay, ay wan minute—my God, why cudn't ye stay?'

'There are so many voices calling me over the sea.'

'Ay, that's thrue.'

He saw them watching him, and he feebly dragged me away from the crowd. He kissed me passionately **again and again. The whistle blew.**

'All aboard!' the guard shouted.

He clutched me tightly and clung to me with the clutch of a drowning man. I had to extricate myself and spring on board. I caught a glimpse of him as the train moved out; despair and a picture of death was on his face. His lips were trembling, and his eyes were full of tears.

A few months later they lowered him to rest beside my mother. I want to go back some day and cover them with a slab of marble, on which their names will be cut, and these words:

'Love is Enough.'